David Croal Thomson, Hablot K. Browne

Life and Labours of Hablot Knight Browne

David Croal Thomson, Hablot K. Browne

Life and Labours of Hablot Knight Browne

ISBN/EAN: 9783337293512

Printed in Europe, USA, Canada, Australia, Japan

Cover: Foto ©Raphael Reischuk / pixelio.de

More available books at **www.hansebooks.com**

LIFE AND LABOURS

OF

HABLÔT KNIGHT BROWNE

"PHIZ"

BY

DAVID CROAL THOMSON

AUTHOR OF "THE LIFE AND WORKS OF THOMAS BEWICK"

With One Hundred and Thirty Illustrations

LONDON
CHAPMAN AND HALL, LIMITED
1884

DEDICATED

TO

THE RIGHT HONOURABLE

ARCHIBALD PHILIP PRIMROSE,

FIFTH

EARL OF ROSEBERY,

WHOSE EARNEST WORDS

OF

EARLY ENCOURAGEMENT

HAVE BEEN

AN INCENTIVE TO MY LABOURS

IN

ART AND LETTERS.

"Phiz." A Teetotal Lecture.

PREFACE.

Trying his paces.

THE Life and Labours of Hablôt Knight Browne may fitly be prefaced by the statement that there is much more to be told about his Labours as an artist than about his Life as a man. The works of "Phiz" in designing and etching form the remarkable part of his career, and that only in which the public is likely to be interested. For this reason the Memoir of the artist's Life occupies but a small portion of this book, while his Labours are dwelt on at greater length and with more detail. Moreover, with the private Life of a contemporary artist it is scarcely desirable to deal, and therefore only the chief incidents of Browne's domestic history are narrated in this volume.

As for the artist's Labours, they, being public property, are discussed on their own merits. I have never thought it the duty of an artist's biographer to express satisfaction with everything done by that artist, or even unduly to advance the merits of his best work and partly ignore that in which he failed. Sooner or later all artists are judged by the intrinsic value of their productions; and it is better at once, even at a little sacrifice of enthusiasm, to endeavour soberly and judiciously to admire that which is lastingly good, and weed out that which is ephemeral and weak.

Very little having been previously written about "Phiz," there is no list of authorities to display; but during the preparation of this volume I have been indebted for assistance and advice to many new as well as old friends. My chief thanks are due to Dr. Edgar Browne, of Liverpool, the eldest son of the artist whose works are herein considered. Dr. Browne supplied much of the material for the Memoir of his father, and also assisted me by the loan of the original sketches used throughout the volume as headpieces, initials, and tailpieces, as well as with other matter of value to the book. Thanks are almost equally due to Mr. Robert Young, whose name so often occurs in the text: to his courtesy and help I am deeply indebted, as much for the loan of letters and sketches as for advice in the first stages of the work. To her Grace the Duchess of St. Albans I have also to give thanks for the ready permission granted to use the unrivalled "Phiz" sketches in her possession. To Mr. Frederick Chapman, Mr. F. W. Cosens, Mr. George Halse, Mr. F. G. Kitton, and Mrs. Westall, I am much indebted for the loan of original drawings, letters, and sketches; also to Messrs. Chapman and Hall, Messrs. George Routledge and Sons, Messrs. Ward and Lock, the proprietors of *The Graphic*, and Messrs. Dalziel Brothers, for the use of steel-plate etchings and wood engravings. I have further specially to acknowledge the assistance of Mr. Thomas Allan Croal, Edinburgh, in the revision of the letterpress; and to thank Mr. F. G. Stephens, Mr. Phipps-Jackson, Mr. James

Thomson, Mr. Arthur Allchin, Mr. J. F. Dexter, Mr. William Sharp, and other friends, for notes and various assistance.

I have endeavoured to obtain accuracy and completeness in every part of this work, and no book-illustration, drawing, or picture has been commented on which has not been carefully examined. But as no previous record has been made of Hablôt Browne's achievements in Art, it is possible that some have been passed over. Indulgence is therefore asked if any important work has been overlooked.

D. C. THOMSON.

London,
August 1st, 1884.

Critic and Authors.

"PHIZ."

The Lamp is out that lighted up the text
    Of DICKENS, LEVER—heroes of the pen.
Pickwick and *Lorrequer* we love, but next
    We place the man who made us see such men
What should we know of *Martin Chuzzlewit*,
    Stern *Mr. Dombey*, or *Uriah Heep*?
Tom Burke of Ours?—Around our hearths they sit,
    Outliving their creators—all asleep.

      No sweeter gift ere fell to man than his
      Who gave us troops of friends—delightful PHIZ!

He is not dead!   There in the picture-book
    He lives with men and women that he drew;
We take him with us to the cozy nook
    Where old companions we can love anew.
Dear boyhood's friend!   We rode with him to hounds;
    Lived with dear *Peggotty* in after years;
Missed in old Ireland where fun knew no bounds;
    At *Dora's* death we felt poor *David's* tears!

      There is no death for such a man—he is
      The spirit of an unclosed book! immortal PHIZ!

PUNCH, July 22nd, 1882.

TABLE OF CONTENTS.

Preface.

Memoir of Hablôt Knight Browne.

LIST OF PLATES.

LIST OF SMALL ILLUSTRATIONS

PRINTED IN THE TEXT.

₊ Fac-similes of other original drawings are used as Initials at the following pages :—17, 19, 21, 22, 23, 24, 28, 29, 34, 57, 60, 66, 80, 94, 107, 109, 110, 118, 124, 128, 135, 141, 147, 149, 172, 184, 189, 197, 216, 225, 226, 232.

MEMOIR.

THERE are few stories to be told of the juvenile days of Hablôt Knight Browne, the future " Phiz" of popular illustration ; though, like the vast majority of artists, he was precocious and showed his talent early. Several anecdotes of his drawing horses' heads in pencil when very young, and doing things of a similar kind that ordinary children do not attempt, have been circulated ; but there is no incident of well-established authenticity, beyond the general notion of his friends and schoolmasters that " he would some day do something remarkable."

According to the parish register of " St. Mary, Lambeth, in the county of Surrey, in the year 1815," Hablôt Knight, the son of William Loder and Katherine Browne, was born on June 11th, 1815, and was shortly afterwards baptised at his father's house. On December the 21st he was publicly christened at St. Mary's, Lambeth, the Reverend Henry White, "Preacher at the Asylum," performing the ceremony. It is further certified that the "quality, trade, or profession" of the father was a merchant, who had his abode in Kennington Lane; and this, we learn otherwise, was in an old Queen Anne house still standing. Hablôt was the ninth son of a family of ten boys and five girls, and there seems to have been some intention of adding Nonus to the other names he received. There was a Septimus, an Octavius, and a Decimus (see illustrated letter, page 26) also in the family. Hablôt was given him in honoured remembrance of one of Napoleon's officers of the Imperial Guard, who fell at Waterloo, and who was engaged to be married to an elder sister of the artist. Knight was after a friend, Admiral Sir John Knight.

The stock from which the artist sprung was eminently well-to-do in the world. His forefathers did not, indeed, come over with the Conqueror, but they came from France all the same. After the Revocation of the Edict of Nantes the Huguenot Brunets were forced to seek a more liberal-spirited country, and they came to England, ultimately settling in Norfolk. Their name they changed to the essentially English cognomen of Browne, but their nature they could not change, and it has been more than once remarked that they seem to have preserved through many generations all the vivacity, the sense of humour, and the artistic perception characteristic of the nation from which they came.

Neither Hablôt Browne's father nor mother was remarkable in a way that could account for the artist's mental development. The drawing faculty was probably inherited from the father's side; Hablôt's uncle, the Rev. John Browne, rector of Hingham, Norfolk, having been a capital amateur painter in oils, and a long way above the average of the professional painters of his time.

Hablôt Browne's mother was a daughter of Colonel Hunter, who lived in or near Oxford. She was a handsome lady, very good-looking, most particular in her notions, and having, it is said, a great idea of her own importance. The artist's father died abroad about 1824, and the family were left rather ill provided for.

Of Hablôt Browne's brothers, Edgar (who died early at Riga, in Russia,) had a remarkable gift for drawing, which, however, he only cultivated as an amusement. Charles became distinguished in India as a general in the Madras Army. He was an eminent linguist and capable of great things, but was destitute of all ambition.*

After the family removed to Euston Square, Hablôt Browne's early taste for drawing took him to the British Museum, and there he made sketches of the Elgin Marbles. His schoolmaster, at a later time, presented him with a complete treatise on the Arts, so that his bent was known and acknowledged at school. This tutor was the Rev. William Haddock, who kept a private establishment at Botesdale, in Suffolk. A strong attachment existed between master and pupil, and the old preceptor used to visit " Phiz " after he became famous, always rejoicing in his successes, which he had confidently predicted.

On his leaving school, the question as to the youth's future career had to be decided. At first it was thought he should study for the Church ; but, after consideration of his talent for drawing, and with a view to develop it, he was made an apprentice, at the expense of Mr. Bicknell,† to Finden, the well-known engraver and pretty book illustrator of fifty years ago. There, like all the other apprentices, he was set for a year to copy designs in outline and to draw from plaster casts.

* This brother resided with his mother for some time at St. Omer, and hence probably arose the mis-statement that Hablôt Browne was educated there. The artist knew very little of France though he could speak French fairly well, and could read it as easily as English. Latin, it may be added, he also knew well ; and he occasionally read an Italian book in the original language.

† The artist's brother-in-law, and owner of many of Turner's finest drawings.

Although in after years Browne took occasional lessons in painting, it was at Finden's that he received the only regular training in artistic work he ever had. Yet no greater mistake could have been made than in apprenticing a youth with the æsthetic temperament of Hablôt Browne to a partly mechanical and always monotonous business like that of an engraver. "Phiz" was eminently original and fanciful, ill-disposed to be bound by any rules and regulations, and this occupation, however suited to the plodding and patient section of the artistic community, was the last to which he ought to have been sent. It is easily believed, therefore, that with engraving after the manner of Finden, Hablôt Browne troubled himself very little. He was faithful enough to go regularly to his workshop, but after a time he only made believe he was drawing, and would sit at his engraver's desk, with its little drawer open, reading a favourite author. A writer with brilliant imagery was his delight, and Shakespeare's poems and "Hudibras" were the books most frequently found in his hands. As he read, even under the eyes of his master, he would make rapid sketches of the scenes as they presented themselves to his mind, and these were often as excellent as the productions of his prime. This was all very wrong, prosaic people will say, but the artistic gift could not be subdued, and the blunder was not so much in Hablôt Browne deceiving his master, as in his guardians binding him to an occupation for which he was totally unfitted by his natural qualifications.

Finden's studio was agreeable enough in its associations, and there Browne made some friends whose companionship lasted through life. Mr. Robert Young, his oldest and most intimate friend, his partner in many speculations, and advocate and admirer on every occasion, was an apprentice there at the same time. Mr. James Stephenson, Mr. Weatherhead, Mr. John Cousen, and the late W. H. Simmonds and Henry Winkles were also amongst the thirty assistants and apprentices engraving in the same rooms. The last-named assistant, Henry Winkles, was a man of parts, and projected a publication on the Cathedrals of England (see Chapter X.), which was ably conducted. Having observed the talent of young Hablôt Browne, he gave him some drawing to do in his spare time. Winkles made an outline of any cathedrals he required to have illustrated, and it was then handed to Browne, who "invested it with artistic merit," adding figures and light and shade to the scene.

Notwithstanding that a certain amount of artistic progress was made and life-long friendships were thus begun, the engraver's business was so unsuited to Browne, that he soon felt it was not possible for him to prosecute it further. He more and more neglected his work; disagreements ensued, and ultimately it was agreed to cancel the indentures. This could hardly have been done without serious consideration. Bicknell, who paid Browne's apprentice fees, was very fond of dealing with engravings as commercial speculations, and was entitled to have some deference paid to his wishes; he was rather annoyed at the seeming perverseness of the young man, but genius and fate were stronger than the will of a patron, and Hablôt Browne left mechanical engraving for good in the year 1834.

Having rapidly sketched the youthful career of the future "Phiz," we now reach the time when he appeared before the world as a personality on his own account. The Society of Arts, in those days, offered prizes for the best work of Art executed in etching or engraving,* and, with a striking similarity to the experience of Thomas Bewick—another celebrated book-illustrator—his first public recognition was by that body. Hablôt Browne had made a clever drawing of John Gilpin, and from this he etched a large plate (about sixteen by ten inches), which in 1833 won a medal as "the best representation of an historical subject." This "historical" subject shows the worthy citizen at full speed in his famous ride, and though the action of the horse is good, the accessories are inadequately treated, and the colour in

* Why the Society does not still do so is not easily told.

the etching is very weak.   There are potentialities in the plate, however,
which make it interesting; and it speaks highly for the artistic acumen of
the Society that in the youthful etcher they divined the world-renowned
" Phiz " of coming years.

The Memoir of Hablôt Browne from the time of
his making illustrations for " Pickwick " is so much
the enumeration of the labours of his long life that
there is not a great deal to be told which the reader
will not find, more appropriately, in the chapters of
this book devoted to their consideration.

It was in the early summer of 1836 that Dickens and " Phiz " first met,
just when the success of the serial publication of " Pickwick " seemed likely
to be wrecked by the want of a good illustrator.   " Nemo " was the title
Hablôt Browne first wrote underneath his etchings.   He had made up his
mind to be a painter, and had no desire to appear before the public as a
" mere book-illustrator."   In the third plate, however, he etched for the novel
he changed his signature to " Phiz," the name which has become famous
to all readers of Dickens's works, and of many of the most popular novels
published between 1836 and 1860.

The origin of the title " Phiz " is very simple, and does not admit of any
elaborate explanation or require a lengthy history.   The artist himself has
told it in a very few words, and to these there is little or nothing to add.   " I
signed myself as 'Nemo' to my first etchings," he said, "before adopting
' Phiz ' as my sobriquet," and this change was made " to harmonize, I
suppose, better with Dickens's ' Boz.' "   It was the artist's fancy to take a
peculiar name, and whether he did so to conceal his identity, hoping always to
achieve what he thought would be more worthy fame as a painter, or simply,
as he says, to correspond with Dickens's " Boz," is a matter really of small
moment.   Having hit on " Phiz " as an easily-remembered title which formed

an artistic-looking signature, he employed it on most of his Dickens illustrations.   Generally speaking, also, it is found on all his better works.   He afterwards frequently used his own name; but, accidentally or designedly, " H. K. B." is most frequently appended to the less excellent productions. In the later volumes of Dickens's novels the letterpress title-page bore " With illustrations by H. K. Browne," but the public never thoroughly grasped the fact that Hablôt Knight Browne and "Phiz" were one and the same person. It was not an uncommon remark during the artist's later life, on the publication of a new book with "engravings after H. K. Browne," to hear people say, " Browne's illustrations are not so good as those of our old friend 'Phiz.'"* It is even likely that if this volume on the Life and Labours of the artist had not his *nom de crayon* prominently marked on the title, some persons would not recognise the comparatively unknown name, Hablôt Knight Browne, as the illustrator they knew so well as "Phiz."

Dickens and Hablôt Browne were always good friends, though the excessive shyness of the artist kept the intimacy from that natural growth the author would gladly have encouraged. In February, 1838, they went together to Yorkshire to see for themselves the schools which Dickens was to describe and "Phiz" to illustrate in "Nicholas Nickleby." In the late autumn of the same year they had another bachelor expedition, when they visited Stratford-on-Avon. Kenilworth, and Warwick.   On November 1st they were at Shrewsbury, and in the evening went to the theatre. Dickens, writing to his wife at the time, said, " It is a good theatre, but the actors are very funny.   Browne laughed with such indecent heartiness at one point of the entertainment that an old gentleman in the next box suffered the most violent indignation."

* It may also he noted as showing the difference of taste, that some people thought " H. K. B." had cut out " Phiz ; " and it is further worth remarking that a few old booksellers think that " Phiz " was George Cruikshank, and advertise books which Browne illustrated under that artist's name.

For many years Dickens and Browne kept up a close correspondence, both in connection with their mutual labours as well as on other subjects. Unfortunately, Browne did not set any store by his letters, and late in life, when on the eve of a household removal, he made a bonfire of his correspondence, burning a large number of letters from Dickens, Lever, Ainsworth, and other writers whose books he illustrated. Some of the letters to Browne still exist, however, and there is none more interesting than the following from Dickens, hitherto unpublished. It is dated 15th March, 1847, and the first part of the letter, which refers to an illustration from "Dombey," is quoted in Chapter II., at page 65. It then proceeds to refer to an incident which requires no explanation :—

"I wish you *had* been at poor Hall's funeral—and I am sure they would have been glad. They seem to have had a delicacy in asking any one not of the family, lest it should be disagreeable. I went myself only after communicating with Chapman, and telling him that I wished to pay that last mark of respect if it did not interfere with their arrangements. He lies in the Highgate Cemetery, which is beautiful. He had a good little wife if ever man had, and the accounts of her tending of him at the last are deeply affecting. Is it not a curious coincidence, remembering our connexion afterwards, that I bought the magazine in which the first thing I ever wrote was published from poor Hall's hands? I have been thinking all day of that, and of that time when the Queen went into the City, and we drank claret (it was in their earlier days) in the counting-house. You remember?

"Charley, thank God, better and better every hour. Don't mind sending me the second sketch. It is so late.—Ever faithfully, my dear Browne, C. D."

In 1840 Browne married Miss Reynolds, a lady who still survives her husband, and who bore him nine children—five boys and four girls. She proved a devoted wife and mother, and the artist's domestic life must be considered to have been eminently satisfactory. In the society of his wife and children— to whom he was fondly attached—his greatest pleasure consisted.

At the birth of his seventh child, in April, 1856, he wrote a humorous letter to Mr. Robert Cole, which Messrs. B. and J. F. Meehan, of Bath, have kindly lent me for insertion :—

"MY DEAR SIR,—Doesn't *the* Pope say something to the effect that 'Man never *is*—but always *to be* blessed!' Although an out-and-out Protestant, a regular Exeter Haller (coming out strong in May!) I am inclined to think he is nearer the mark than the man (David or Sol.?) who sings about the blessed state of the man with a perambulator—quiver full, I mean!

"*He* must have been peeping through a crack in the shutter of the future and had a glimpse of some of his descendants with *bags* full of 'Old clo! clo!! clo!!!' 'Happy is the man who has his bag full, &c., &c.,' having no suspicion all the time of double income-tax!

"However, many thanks for all kind enquiries. My wife, with the little addition to the quiver, are doing well, and '*I* am as well as can be expected.'

"With kind regards to your daughters and thanks for their con—do—len—ces,

"I am, dear Sir,

He lived after marriage at a house in Howland Street, near Tottenham Court Road, London, shortly afterwards removing to Stamford Villas,

Fulham Road. The letter reproduced below—from the collection of Mr. W. C. Gilles—was written from this residence. It was addressed to Decimus Browne, the artist's brother, and it mentions Mr. Robert Young as one of the "odd fish at table." It also shows how ready the artist was with his pen to convey in a few strokes far more than a lengthy note would give. The watch-dog at the kennel beside the rough sketch of his own residence at Stamford Villas is clever, the size of the dog-kennel humorously indicating his sense of the diminutive character of his little home. He always retained the idea that there was something comical in a little house. The dancing pudding is one of the funniest little sketches he ever did and is used on the cover of this book.

From Fulham, whither the family had moved for Mrs. Browne's health, another removal—and for the same reason—was made to Croydon about 1846. They had two houses at Croydon—one Thornton House, a queer rambling old place, consisting of two small houses knocked into one; the second a new "villa residence" on Duppas Hill.

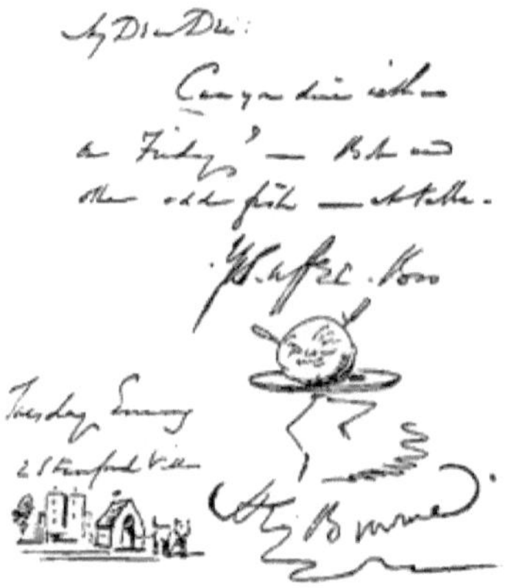

Thornton House possessed ample accommodation for stabling, and a superfluity of outhouses that suited Browne's taste. Here he made himself happy, installing a couple of horses for regular use. Hitherto he had only been able to indulge his passion for hunting intermittently, though he seems to have acquired and found means to gratify the taste as a mere lad, either by hiring or borrowing steeds. At this Croydon house he seems to have settled down by degrees into a quiet routine of life, with less and less inclination for society or sightseeing. From the first he would have nothing to do with local society; and as local society was anxious to have something to do with him, his notoriety became a source of annoyance to him. For many years there was a sort of open house on Sundays, and friends from London—many known to fame—made their way down by road or by the curious "atmospheric railway," just then running its brief career. So long as the society consisted of his intimates he was happy enough; but, as is the case with many men of genius, a stranger, or one whom he fancied to be unsympathetic, was sure to affect him unfavourably. This shyness, which afterwards became a marked feature in his character, is the more remarkable as he possessed in a large degree those gifts which make a man shine in society. At Duppas Hill there was no stable, and Browne never settled in it, removing shortly afterwards to Banstead, where he was completely happy. But at Banstead he was so far away that fewer people visited him, and as he went nowhere, he dropped out of the knowledge of the artistic community of the metropolis. Besides, new people would not come to a place where they had to be met by appointment, and driven over a bleak moor.

At Christmas, 1859, he returned to London, going to Horbury Crescent, where he remained several years. In 1865, Blenheim Crescent was his residence; in 1872, No. 99, Ladbroke Grove Road, and finally, in 1880 he removed to Brighton.

In September, 1845, Charles Lever invited "Phiz" to go with him a ramble through Switzerland and the Tyrol, offering, as an inducement, to drive the artist with his own nags. To this liberal invitation "Phiz" replied that he "had just had a sort of holiday, and must buckle to again, and work, work, work." And he sent the author some illustrations for the "Knight of Gwynne" and promised to do his best endeavours to co-operate with Lever to make all the men brave, but the task of making the women virtuous he said he must leave to the writer.

Just before the publication of "Jack Hinton," in 1844, Browne was invited, with Samuel Lover —who was to paint a miniature of Lever—to go to Brussels, and in the Life of Lever this is recorded in some detail. Lever wanted "Phiz" to have the characters described to him personally, and the illustrator made the sketches for "Jack Hinton" under Lever's eye. Lever at the same period wrote to MacGlashan, his publisher, that "Phiz" seemed disposed to take much more pains than he did with "Charles O'Malley," and that both artist and author were quite in heart about them. The revels in Lever's house during the visit were hearty enough. They held an installation of the "Knights of Alcantara," Lover, Lever, and "Phiz" being made Grand Crosses of the Order, with "music, procession, and a grand ballet to conclude: they did nothing all day, and in some instances all night, but eat, drink, and laugh." Before separating, Lever made Browne promise to go to Dublin with him so that he could see "Paddy *au naturel*," and not "that wretched misrepresentation of him that St. Giles's offers"—an expedition that was fruitful to "Phiz" in giving him new ideas.

Lever's biographer mentions that during this visit "Phiz" and Lever "for the first time had become sworn allies, having arranged on an admirable footing all their future operations." Further on, however, he records that Lever wrote of the illustrations to "Jack Hinton," that "Browne's sketches are as usual caricatures, and make my scenes really too riotous and disorderly. The character of my books for uproarious people and incidents I owe mainly to Master ' Phiz ; ' " while a little later Lever thought of starting a newspaper with him, *The Weekly Quiz*, with illustrations by " Phiz."

In October, 1847, Browne was once more in Ireland, this time with Mr. Robert Young. It was just after the terrible potato famine, and the artist and his friend were introduced to Mitchell and many other revolutionary characters. Carleton, whose books " Phiz " illustrated, Browne met for the first time at the publishers, Duffy and MacGlashan, and laid the foundation of many business transactions for the future. It was during this visit (and not during the first one, as has been stated) that a large series of sketches of Irish character were produced, as referred to in our second chapter on Browne's water-colour drawings. The two travellers went to Wicklow, and then across the island by Bianconi's cars to Galway and Connemara. They also visited the scenes of Lever's " Knight of Gwynne," but beyond the experience obtained in seeing the Irish people as they really were, there was no practical gain to Browne's reputation at the time, as no use was made of the sketches.

ABLÔT BROWNE was in every sense of the word a bad business man. From this Irish trip he could easily have produced the series of etchings he contemplated, and have gained largely in worldly position, as it is quite certain they would have paid as a commercial speculation. But he failed to catch the right moment, and soon the time went by when success could be assured. " Phiz " never made a large income, and unwisely never raised his prices. He was paid no more for the " Knight of Gwynne " or " Dombey " than he was for " Lorrequer " and " Pickwick." Fifteen guineas was his price at first for an etching, and though—as in the Smedley plates—he often took less, he never seems to have asked more. He never knew what he earned or what he spent, and would for many years take no thought of it. When he wanted money he applied to any publisher who happened to owe him something, and it was unlucky for the employer if he could not instantly settle the account; for Browne never would, or perhaps never could, understand why he should not have his money the very day his work was completed.

From the time of "Pickwick" until he went to Banstead, he was decidedly a prosperous man, always earning sufficient for his simple wants. At Croydon he was usually very busily occupied with etchings, and he easily sold such drawings or pictures as he could find time to paint. When he moved to Banstead he was out of the way of everybody. Etching as a means of illustrating had gone out of favour, or was rapidly decreasing, and as the charms of painting unfolded themselves to him he became careless of his book-illustrations, and thus his income fell off considerably. When he returned to London he was at first pressed for money, but in a short period he had put his affairs in good order; and at the time of a serious illness, in 1867, he had increased his income, and had a considerable number of commissions in hand. After this illness he made very little money, and towards the end of his life literally nothing. Probably had he not broken down so comparatively early—at the age of fifty-two—he would have managed to live as most Bohemian financiers do, sometimes full of cash and full of happiness, at other times "hard up" and rather doleful. As matters were with him, however, he found himself as age approached face to face with the most serious difficulty in life for a family man—the want of money and the lack of ability whereby to bring it in. Browne was never really in straits till after his illness. Sometimes he had a few hundreds in the cupboard, which anybody else would have invested; but his general habit was to order the things he wanted, and then set to work to pay for them. Whilst health lasted he was always able to do this with ease and certainty. On returning to London, however, his occupation as a book-illustrator was gone. He had separated from Dickens, and other authors were betaking themselves to magazines, instead of publishing in a serial form. He set himself to work—drew on wood, in graphotype (which he detested), lithographed hunting scenes, &c., and began to have a very good sale for his water-colours. He did a great deal of work, and in 1866 must have made a considerable income.

The direct cause of his monetary difficulties was his failing health. This greatly impaired his artistic capabilities, and they gradually became less estimable until the time of his death in 1882. As early as 1867 he had sustained a severe shock of a kind of paralysis, and for the remaining fifteen years of his life he never was the same man again, either as a designer or as a draughtsman. This illness in 1867 is said to have been partly caused by his having slept in a draught in a seaside house, but from a medical description of the disease there appears to have been some blood-poisoning; and the main symptom that afterwards caused his death was inflammation of the spinal cord (myelitis). Dr. Westall, in whom he had implicit faith, attended him, but it is possible that the serious nature of the disease was not understood until its sad results were seen.

After five months of great suffering he sat up and began to draw. He was not really convalescent, but his active nature asserted itself, and he persisted in working, in spite of advice to the contrary. His perseverance was little short of madness. When he first began, the perspiration would pour off him after half an hour's exertion, and then he had to lay by his work and rest again. He refused to go to the seaside, asserting that his health was returning and that he had a great deal of back-way to make up.

From the first it was seen that this illness had fatally shattered him, beyond hope of recovery. When attacked he was an active, vigorous man of middle age with remarkable fertility of brain and facility of hand. There was no sign of serious impairment of power. He had never been known to have a day's illness in his life. But a space of less than half a year sufficed to reduce him to the condition of a broken down old man. He left the sick room with white hair, pallid complexion, and a partial paralysis of the right arm and leg. It is characteristic of the man that he never complained nor admitted that he was ill. He persisted in calling the loss of power in his limbs "rheumatism," and evidently to within a short period of his death thought it was curable. To the end he was somewhat surprised at the cessation of a demand for his work, and never realised that his hand had lost its cunning.

In his later years Browne was ever (to use his own words) "in a pickle of some sort or another," and occasionally he was under extreme pressure for want of funds. In a letter written on March 15th, 1879, he complains justly of the coldheartedness of certain rich relations who declined to assist him, and says, "I don't know where to turn or what to do. I have at last come to a full stop, and don't see my way just yet to get on again. My occupation seems gone, extinct; I suppose I am thought to be used up, and I have been long enough before the public. I have not had a single thing to do this year, nor for some months previous in the past year." Is it possible to conceive a more pathetic picture of the latter days of a once popular artist?

In the July before this (1878), Mr. Luke Fildes, A.R.A., and one of Browne's best friends in his later days, suggested that the artist should apply to Government for a pension, and Browne prepared the following memorandum to be employed in proper form for a petition :—

"I am sixty-three years old, and have been before the public forty-five years as an artist, constantly illustrating from month to month all sorts of books and authors—Bulwer, Dickens, Lever, Ainsworth, and many others; magazines, papers, periodicals of all sorts, comic and serious. It is just possible I have helped to amuse a few in my time, and in my earlier days I was a bit of a favourite, I think, but the present generation 'knoweth not Joseph.' I have had a large family, nine still living—four girls and one boy still dependent on me. I have had one paralytic attack, and I have been blinded of one eye for five months by acute rheumatism, but I am all right now."

This note was sent to Mr. Young, who prepared the petition, but unfortunately the result was unfavourable. Even at such a crisis, when the whole world seemed turned against him, the artist's humour did not altogether forsake him, as we find him writing as follows on July 28th, 1878, to Mr. Young, when sending the memorandum :—

"Many thanks for the 'petition'—it seems the correct thing. If Dizzy is benign, I shall henceforth become his steady supporter and a true Conservative (of the pension) as long as I live."

Browne we see was ever hopeful, even in the midst of his worst pecuniary troubles. In 1878 he again writes, "Things are as bad as they can be; so I suppose, as 'it is a long lane that has no turning,' my luck will turn sooner or later. Somehow, in spite of the black look of things, I have a sort of conviction that I shall die tolerably '*comfortable*.' However, *faith* is a great thing, isn't it, my boy? "

Although Browne still looked for a restoration of health with a sort of phenomenal cheerfulness, that was not his only point of resemblance to Mr. Micawber. In money matters, his friends perceived clearly that his income from his works had almost ceased, and owing chiefly to the representations of Messrs. Frith, Fildes, and Wells, the Royal Academy awarded him an annuity. He was greatly pleased with this unexpected assistance, especially as it was conveyed to him with the assurance that it had been awarded to him in recognition of his distinguished services to Art. Free from vanity as he was, he certainly derived considerable satisfaction from the thought that he was not altogether forgotten.

One of the things he began on his recovery was the Household Edition of Dickens. In the feeble and childish scrawls of those blocks may be seen the injury that had been inflicted. He recovered a good deal after that, but he never had complete power over his right leg, and he could not make the forefinger and thumb of the right hand meet. So greatly was the power of the right hand impaired, that he had to support it by the left in order to get a glass to his mouth in drinking. Hence he was obliged to hold the pencil or brush in an extraordinary and clumsy fashion, and his drawing was executed by a sort of sweeping movement of the whole arm.   He had to be propped up in certain positions against his table in order to get at his work. If he moved without help he was likely to fall down.   Nobody looking at him could have supposed him capable of drawing, and the wonder was not that the work was bad, but that it was done at all.   His invention and fancy before that, which were simply inexhaustible—as shown both in conversation and in the numerous schemes for publication, of which many men would have made fortunes—decayed rapidly.   He seems to have *remembered* fancies and designs of earlier dates, and executed them in his feeble fashion ; but there is nothing he appears to have distinctly originated after that.   In fact he had a serious though partial destruction of spinal cord and brain, and in all these cases there is a strong tendency for degeneration to spread directly and by reflex far beyond the centres originally attacked. Very early he lost his colour sense, which he always said had been much injured by continual working at the steel or in black and white.

His affliction gradually became more pronounced, and on the 8th of July, 1882, he died at the age of sixty-seven.   On the 14th all that was mortal of the artist was laid in its last resting-place on the summit of the hill on the northern side of the extra-mural cemetery at Brighton.

ALTHOUGH Hablôt Browne had a serious defect in his character, yet, as it is one that most artists have a tendency to and many never overcome, the world very soon forgives and forgets it. To be a bad business man and often in need of ready money are no crimes ; and if the artist may have been blameable in not providing better for old age, the fault was bitterly atoned for in life, and should not be charged against him after death.   His excellent qualities far outweighed anything of an opposite tendency, and it is remarkable, bearing in mind how irritable ill health and lack of funds make most people, that his amiability and modesty survived his period of success and never deserted him to the day of his death. In the following brief tribute, written by a member of his household, some insight into his personally loving and estimable character will be obtained :—

" His life was always quiet, one day so much like another, and the greater part of each spent in his own room, alone with his thoughts and his pencil. About half-past eight he would come down to breakfast, read the newspaper, and then regularly disappear into his own room until dinner-time. After dinner he generally remained in the dining-room reading, and if not reading he would be sure to be working. He was seldom idle, and even his evenings were spent in reading or working. He was much affected by the weather, and gloried in bright sunshiny days; a dreary, wet, gloomy day had a most depressing effect upon him, and in Ladbroke Grove Road he frequently went to bed in the afternoon, unless he drew down the blinds and lit up the gas to shut out the gloominess. He was most simple in his ways and life, and hated affectation of any kind, most careless of dress or personal appearance, and did not care in the least what he looked like, or what people would think of him, never studying Mrs. Grundy. Few men thought so little of food as he did, or ate so little. He also had a dislike to asking for anything or being waited upon, was very independent always, and never complained even when he felt ill, or made the slightest fuss about himself in any way. He was particularly kind and fond of animals, especially horses and dogs. If he found the cat in his armchair he would never disturb her, however tired he was, but would inconvenience himself for her sake, saying, " Let her be, poor pussy, she likes that chair." He never was haughty or abrupt to poor people who addressed him out of doors, and was as polite to them as he would be to the wealthy. He was a great lover of the sea, and of all that was wild and grand in nature; he used often to tell us how grandly the sea broke in upon the west coast of Ireland. He was interested in astronomy too, and said he should like to be an astronomer, if he were a rich man and hadn't to work for his living."

When on any of the few excursions he made to the country, it was his custom to write long letters home describing the places and people he was visiting, emphasizing the written account with sketches of whatever struck him as interesting. He visited the Isle of Man about 1865, and sent a long illustrated letter to his son Walter minutely describing the character of the locality. One of the sketches is peculiarly instructive as showing how rapidly Browne could grasp the feeling of the scene and bring it clearly to the eye.

This sketch of rocks is drawn in the letter a little larger size than here reproduced. The accumulation of heavy masses of rocks is drawn with a

boldness and accuracy which has few parallels in similar or even in more carefully executed work. In it there is no fuss; it is only a simple illustration from a father to a son of something which has struck the artist. He describes the rocks as looking like books that have been tumbled out, and did not resist the temptation to give his recollections of them, his hasty pen having, in a few lines, rendered his idea of the forms which had impressed him. Here we see the artist and draughtsman completely off his guard. Here he is not—as every painter does, and must do to a certain extent—posing for effect. The rocks are strange, weird, and fascinating to one who has spent so much time in the man-made cities. The God-made rocks have fairly startled him, and every line tells of his excited feelings. The impression of gloom he has received from these mighty rocks pervades his letter; for once he fails to become humorous, and the feeble efforts to make jokes only serve to contrast with the general tone of the didactic epistle. The sketch may seem slight enough, but a careful study of it reveals much power of pencil as well as of observation. For the benefit of the artistically trained reader I give it as a sample of the power of the artist.

From the first Browne always kept out of the way of conversational people, and he thus had fewer acquaintances than artists usually have whose names are in every one's mouth. As already mentioned, " Phiz " was intimate with Lever, and up to about 1851 they used to go about together, Lever's dash probably neutralizing Browne's shyness. Maclise, Patric Park, R.S.A., sculptor, Lucas, a fashionable portrait-painter, and George Bullock were friends; and Mr. Horace Jones, the present London City Architect, was also a frequent visitor. Dr. Westall, of Croydon, the artist's medical attendant, was also an attached and trusted friend. When Dr. Westall's only son died, Browne shut himself up for three days, so as not to be disturbed by any impression, and painted a portrait from memory. It is necessarily slight, but it gives an excellent likeness of the lad. This is typical of the way he then used nature—always from memory. He had no idea, or had lost it, of searching for light and shade—hence the great technical defects of his works—but he sought to reproduce an impression. After he took to shutting himself up, the impression became less and less visual and more and more intellectual. He cared but little for the drawing and colouring of his work. The idea, either comic or pathetic, the conceit or sequence of events became the first consideration. His art, in short, drifted into the border lands between painting and literature. He had no experience in painting a portrait from a model. Moreover, nothing could persuade him to show people his studio, and he took as much trouble to hide himself and his method of working as artists nowadays do to keep themselves *en évidence.*

In almost every lengthy letter he wrote Browne made sketches, and the small four-page letter to the artist's friend, Mr. George Halse, here printed, may be taken as a fair sample of many letters he wrote.

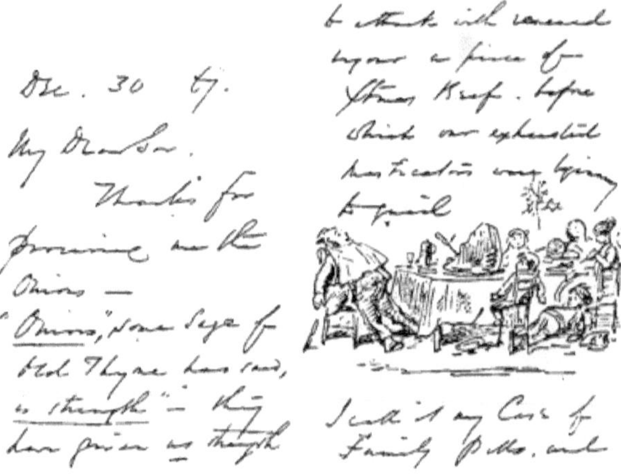

Letter from "Phiz" to Mr. George Halse.

Hablôt Browne was a man of much quietness as regards the serious questions of religious faith. Like many other artists, he seldom or never went to church; yet he had a great fondness for the New Testament, combined with a pronounced dislike of the Old. He seldom worked on Sunday, holding it to be a day of rest, and would never permit any noise or games

by his children on that day. He generally loitered about in the fields, at
the paddock at Croydon or Banstead, or in his own garden. In the afternoon
he generally read. When he removed to London he usually took a walk to
Wormwood Scrubs, or in that direction.

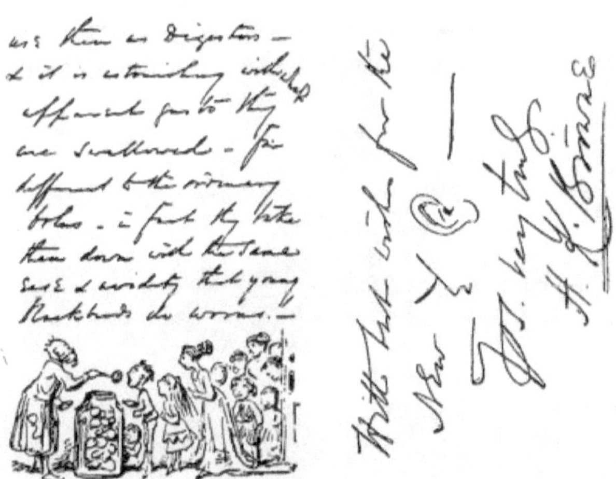

Letter from "Phiz" to Mr. George Halse.—(Continued.)

In personal appearance Hablôt Browne was decidedly well-favoured. In
later years his friends recollect him as an old man, bent and worn with care
and suffering; but in earlier days, and at the time when his admirers love to
think of him, he had a merry twinkle in his eye, a face full of expression,
with blonde curly hair, and a manner courteous, kind, and obliging, having

none of that roughness often affected by artists; innately a gentleman, and with only too much meekness to be financially successful in treading his way through life. That he was thoroughly successful as an illustrator it is the purport of the following chapters to show.

A Portrait of "Phiz." By permission of the Proprietors of *The Graphic*.

"Beginning."

CHAPTER I.

"PHIZ" AS AN ILLUSTRATOR—THE ART OF ILLUSTRATION.

THERE is no doubt that, to the world at large, Hablôt Knight Browne is best known as "Phiz," an illustrator of books. As an artist in oil-colours he would have gained a reputation as a painstaking and decidedly original worker; and, as a sketcher in water-colours, he sometimes showed indications of a capacity which, had it received careful training, would have carried him far into popularity and lasting fame. But notwithstanding his frequent wish to leave "the illustrating business," it is certain that it was only by his book illustrations he could have achieved special distinction. He had received no technical knowledge of the manipulation of colours, and never took pains to obtain it; therefore he was not, strictly speaking, a painter. His power lay in what many lack who quickly overcome the mechanical difficulties of painting—he was gifted with imagination and power of realisation of the highest order. He was an

F

illustrator first, and afterwards, but only afterwards, a painter of consider-
able attainments. He could conceive an idea, and carry it out in black and white, more readily than any man of his time. Or, having received a general impression of what was wanted for the illustration of a story, he could make manifest in a few minutes a composition which would faithfully reflect his conception. He had no difficulty in producing on paper the ideas of his brain, and at his best time his skill never faltered when he had the pencil between his fingers. He had but to think, to be able to express; to desire, to be able to fulfil.

"Phiz" is also characterised by the public as a "funny man" amongst illustrators. In early days he so often made illustrations of humorous incidents that he has been dubbed—and that quite fairly—a man likely to raise a laugh.

Letter (continued) addressed to Dr. Westall ("Phiz's" medical man).

Probably if any disappointment is felt about the illustrations which embellish this book, it will be because—notwithstanding their number — there is not enough of the comic element intermingled. But it is the business of Hablôt Browne's biographer to show that while he is unrivalled in his representations of rollicking humour and exuberant fun, he also was an artist of the serious and almost the gravest side of human life. It appears sometimes to be necessary to man's nature to be evenly balanced in these matters, and when a vein of merriment is granted so also is an equalising fund of melancholy. While Grimaldi was able to be the drollest of beings at one time, he was also the most depressed at others. The airiest-minded people are occasionally the dreariest of companions: their light-heartedness sometimes leaves them, and the pendulum swings to the opposite extreme—from levity into deep gloom. Such a man was Hablôt Browne. As shown by his letters, no man was more easily buoyed up with pleasure or carried away by the frolic of the moment; but occasionally he wandered into the valley of the shadow of death, and imagined and portrayed scenes the very opposite of the mirthful episodes so indelibly associated with his name.

Hablôt Browne's designs have become familiar to all readers of the works of Charles Dickens. They are so thoroughly part of the best of them, that we sometimes do not pay due attention to the masterly descriptions in the text, but look at the plates, grasp the characters, and are satisfied. Charles Dickens has had many illustrators, and some are very formidable rivals of Browne, but, on the whole, no one comes so near the realisation of Dickens's slightly overdrawn characters as "Phiz;" and the creator of Sam Weller, little David Copperfield, Guppy, Squeers, Micawber, Tom Pinch, Major Bagstock, with a dozen others, was a quite worthy fellow-labourer with the greatest novelist of the day. Other illustrators have given us the chief actors in Dickens's novels, but it is through Phiz's work we remember them; and, indeed, subsequent draughtsmen have felt this so powerfully that no one can draw the figures successfully except on the basis of Hablôt Browne's designs.

The same may be said of the drawings for Lever's and Ainsworth's books. These are not so well known as Dickens's more powerful works, but their characters were created by "Phiz," and they can never be otherwise adequately rendered. Lever's and Ainsworth's fiction is less popular than Dickens's, but Hablôt Browne's illustrations are equal in merit in both; and

in several instances the lesser-known volumes contain the more artistically
excellent illustrations.

The Two Chestnuts. From Lever's "Charles O'Malley." Lent by Mr. John Dicks.

An illustration to a story is not by any means such an easy task to a
good draughtsman as might at first be supposed. One naturally believes
that if the writer minutely and carefully describes a scene, and in such
a way that it rises to the mind's eye without difficulty, the artist can have
little or no trouble. This is, however, a mistake. It may be taken for
granted generally in illustration that the more minutely the writer describes
the scene and its surroundings, the more difficult will it be for the artist
to give effect to the description. If a writer marks the principal characters

well, that is, describes them so as to unite individuality with precise detail, and leaves the remainder of the incident in what artists call "mystery," then the task of the illustrator is comparatively easy. But when the author enters into details, and describes with care what he wishes to impress on the reader, the labour of the draughtsman rises in proportion. The artist has to be careful to follow all the points brought forward by the writer, and he has to see that each detail is subordinated to the whole, so that a work of pictorial art be produced as well as a work of simple pictorial illustration. When the author is precise the illustrator has to be particular; when the writer is vague the artist may be free.

Take, for instance, as an example of the difficulties of the draughtsman, the illustration to " David Copperfield" of which phases are here given. Of this I am fortunate enough, by permission of Her Grace the Duchess of St. Albans, to be able to reproduce the two original pencil drawings. For this Dickens described the scene very carefully :—

"I watched her [my Aunt Betsy], with my heart at my lips, as she marched up to a corner of her garden, and stooped to dig up some little root there. Then, without a scrap of courage, but with a deal of desperation, I went softly in and stood beside her, touching her with my finger.

" ' If you please, ma'am,' I began.

" She started and looked up.

" ' If you please, aunt.'

" ' Eh !' exclaimed Miss Betsy, in a tone of amazement I have never heard approached.

" ' If you please, aunt, I am your nephew !'

" ' Oh, Lord !' said my aunt. And she sat flat down in the garden-path.

" ' I am David Copperfield, of Blunderstone, in Suffolk—where you came, on the night when I was born, and saw my dear mamma. I have been very unhappy since she died. I have been slighted, and taught nothing, and thrown upon myself, and put to work not fit for me. It made me run away to you. I was robbed at first setting out, and have walked all the way, and have never slept in a bed since I began the journey.' Here my self support gave way all at once; and with a movement of my hands, intended to show her my ragged state, and call it to

Nº 1

witness that I had suffered something, I broke into a passion of crying, which I suppose had been pent up within me all the week.

"My aunt, with every sort of expression but wonder discharged from her countenance, sat on the gravel, staring at me, until I began to cry; when she got up in a great hurry, collared me, and took me into the parlour."

In the first sketch for the Plate we have the artist following the direction of the writer, and with the disastrous result that though the drawing is loyal to the text, as an artistic production it is ridiculous. No lady could look anything but foolish sitting on the ground as described, though it does not appear so absurd when we read about the inelegant attitude. Dickens saw at a glance that the drawing would not do, so another was prepared and submitted to him as usual. This is the second design for the Plate. Still, however, the author is dissatisfied, for now the boy has lost some of the charm he was endowed with in the first, and the background is not so well composed. The artist, therefore, combines the two designs, takes the figure of David from one and of "my Aunt Betsy" from the other, and intermingling the backgrounds, produces the etching which was used in the publication. We do not stay meanwhile to consider the other merits of the illustration, but may point to the little sketch at the corner of the second drawing, where the whole incident is caricatured so unmercifully.

Again in "Mrs. Gamp proposes a toast," the next Plate, we have an illustration which takes an enormous amount of consideration before the drawing includes all the details mentioned in the text:—

"The bed itself was decorated with a patchwork quilt of great antiquity. . . . Some rusty gowns and other articles of that lady's wardrobe depended from the posts, and these had so adapted themselves by long usage to her figure that more than one impatient husband coming in precipitately at about the time of twilight, had been for an instant stricken dumb by the supposed discovery that Mrs. Gamp had hanged herself. One gentleman coming on the usual hasty errand, had said indeed that they looked like guardian angels 'watching over her in sleep.' But that, as Mrs. Gamp said, 'was his first;' and he never repeated the sentiment though he often repeated the visit.

" The chairs in Mrs. Gamp's apartment were extremely large and broad-backed, which was more than a sufficient reason for there being but two in number. They were both elbow-chairs of ancient mahogany, and were chiefly valuable for the slippery nature of their seats, which had been originally horsehair, but were now covered with a slimy substance of a bluish tint, from which the visitor began to slide away with a dismayed countenance immediately after sitting down.

" What Mrs. Gamp wanted in chairs she made up in bandboxes; of which she had a great collection devoted to the reception of various miscellaneous valuables, which were not, however, as well protected as the good woman, by a pleasant fiction, seemed to think; for though every bandbox had a carefully closed lid, not one among them had a bottom, owing to which cause the property within was merely, as it were, extinguished. The chest of drawers having been originally made to stand upon the top of another chest, had a dwarfish, elfin look alone; but in regard of its security, it had a great advantage over the bandboxes, for as all the handles had been long ago pulled off, it was very difficult to get at its contents. This indeed was only to be done by one of two devices, either by tilting the whole structure forward until all the drawers fell out together, or by opening them singly with knives, like oysters.

" Mrs. Gamp stored all her household matters in a little cupboard by the fireplace; beginning below the surface (as in nature) with the coals, and mounting gradually upwards to the spirits, which, from motives of delicacy, she kept in a teapot. The chimney-piece was ornamented with a small almanack, marked here and there in Mrs. Gamp's own hand, with a memorandum of the date at which some lady was expected to fall due. It was also embellished with three profiles, one in colours of Mrs. Gamp herself in early life; one, in bronze of a lady in feathers, supposed to be Mrs. Harris, as she appeared when dressed for a ball; and one in black of Mr. Gamp, deceased. The last was full-length, in order that the likeness might be rendered more obvious and forcible by the introduction of the wooden leg.

" A pair of bellows, a pair of pattens, a toasting-fork, a kettle, a pap-boat, a spoon for the administration of medicine to the refractory, and lastly, Mrs. Gamp's umbrella, which as something of great price and rarity was displayed with particular ostentation, completed the decorations of the chimney-piece and adjacent wall.

*   *   *   *   *   *   *

" When the meal came to a termination (which it was pretty long in doing) and Mrs. Gamp having cleared away, produced the teapot from the top shelf, simultaneously with a couple of wine-glasses, they were quite amiable.

" ' Betsey,' said Mrs. Gamp, filling her own glass, and passing the teapot, ' I will now propose a toast. My frequent pardiner, Betsey Prig !'

" ' Which, altering the name to Sairah Gamp, I drink,' said Mrs. Prig, ' with love and tenderness.' "

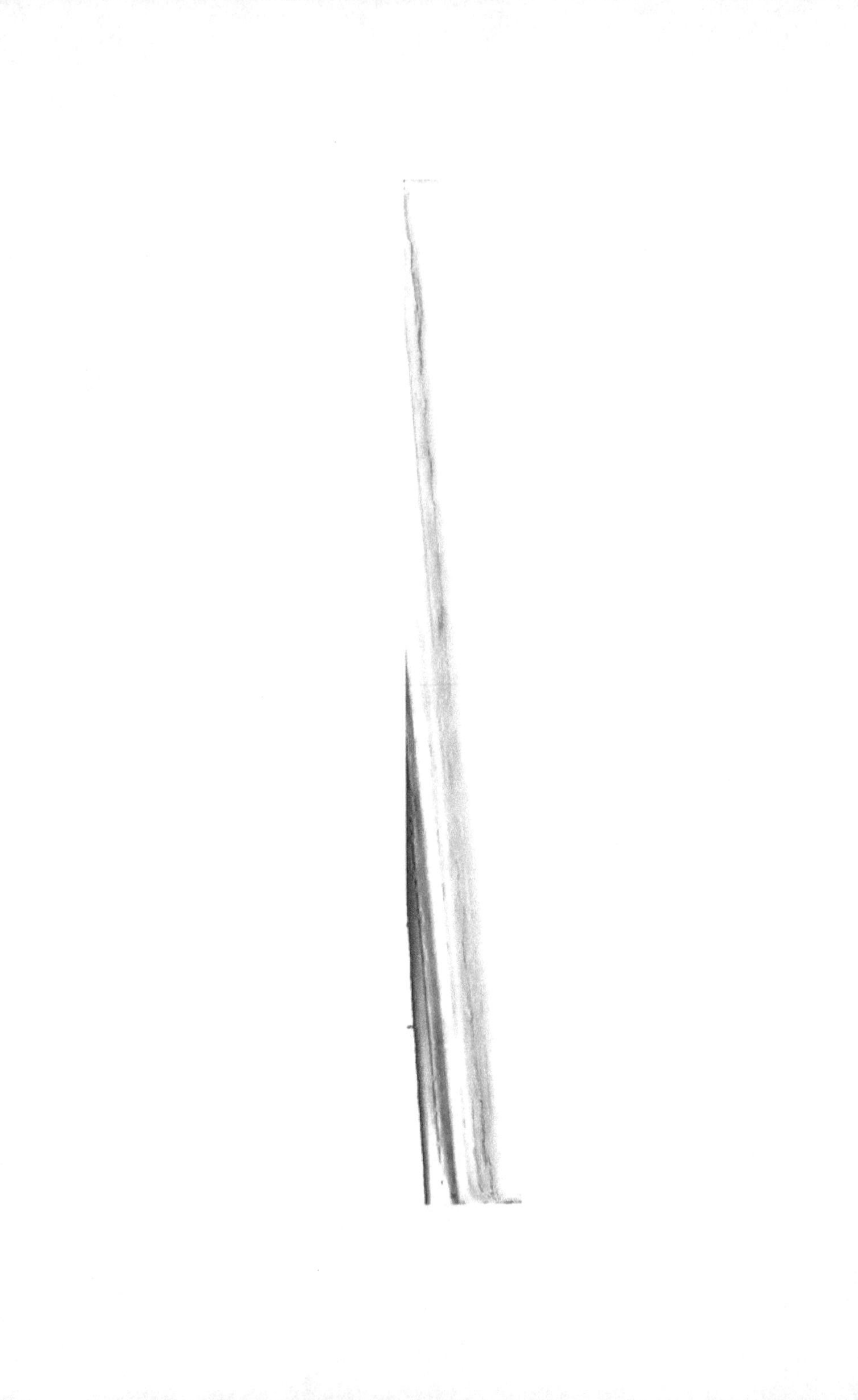

HE writer and artist in an ideal illustration should work together towards similar but not identical ends. The author should not seek to invade the province of the draughtsman by too curious particulars of shape and surroundings, all of which probably cannot be taken into one view of the scene. The artist not hindering the labour of the author by failing to bring out the points on which insistence has been made, but rather stimulating the thought of the reader, so that he realises more completely the writer's language. The illustrator is not to try to be a simple follower of directions laid down, any more than an engraver on steel of a large work can exactly imitate the chiaroscuro, in black and white, of the colourist, but is compelled to accentuate here and subordinate there. As in the engraver's case so with the illustrator; as the Art of the painter is different from that of the worker with the needle, so is the Art of the author different from that of the artistic draughtsman. The same rules do not and can not apply in both instances; so that as each works towards the same general end but by vastly different means, so must each be left to follow that route which seems to him best. The illustrator's duty is primarily to enhance the interest of a literary production, and if he fails in this he fails fatally; and even when he does add interest his difficulties are by no means over, as his artistic powers must be brought into play to see that while he makes an enhancement to the letterpress he does not offend against any of the canons of Art and good taste.

It is in this that the illustrations of " Phiz " are eminently successful. They help the text and they are good works of Art. It was not so much as a precise realist that Browne succeeded best, but because his designs partook more of the character of being pleasant comments on the text and not irritants to the reader. Besides this, they do not too greedily claim praise for themselves. So long as the reader is occupied with the merit of the story, he is not reminded annoyingly of the personality of the illustrator; just as, in the same way, one does not in well-written books find the author too obtrusive. And if it be wise in the writer to seek to sink himself in the narrative he is producing, so is this even far more important for the illustrator. As a general rule the draughtsman must subordinate himself and remain subordinate to the author, for the all-sufficient reason that it is always more advisable for the illustrator to follow the ideas of the writer, than for the author to have to " write up" to the illustrations.

To continue this argument: as a reader, after he has read the letterpress then begins to think of the writer, so also he looks at the illustrations, and, recalling the narrative, criticises favourably or adversely the designer's work. And it is worth remarking how unanimous people are as to the qualities of an illustration. Those who would not dare to place themselves as critics before a painting and give expression to their ideas concerning it, never hesitate to praise or condemn an illustration. Before the merest daub on canvas they may be silent, feeling their incapacity to judge truly of its merits; but give them a bad illustration, and though they profess ignorance of Art, they will heartily and judiciously condemn an unworthy production. Take as an instance poor Buss's two illustrations for " Pickwick."* Did any one ever say a good word for them? Any child who can read will condemn them as bad; although it is to be observed this failure is not so much because of their lack of artistic power—which is very apparent—but because the entire sentiment of the writer is missed, and the expressions fail to satisfy the mind of the reader who has just read the description.

" Phiz" was peculiarly successful in this, the *raison d'être* of illustration. In his hundreds of illustrations he seldom or never failed to realise thoroughly what the reader desired most to see pictorially represented. That he did always succeed would be to say he was more than mortal. He was not, for instance, always successful in pleasing the rightly fastidious Charles Dickens, but he never missed the mark altogether, as Buss did; and his

* See Chapter III.

illustrations are always helps to the proper understanding of the text, and never a hindrance.

It is to be noted also that "Phiz" never shirked grappling with the illustration of a complicated scene because of its difficulty of interpretation. In the wide and ever-extending work of illustration of the present day we frequently come across both books and periodicals, lavishly got up, with illustrations which decidedly hint of their draughtsman shirking his work. It is now a common experience for the readers of illustrated novels to have some trouble in finding the part of the letterpress which refers to the drawing accompanying it. Do we not sometimes find the illustrations to belong to some obscure passage having little or nothing to do with the main story; and is this not done because the draughtsmen have found difficulty in coming up to the conception the public is quite able to form; and, rather than risk being condemned as unskilful interpreters, they choose to be grumbled at as being unwise in their choice of scene?

Far different was it with "Phiz." His earliest illustrations were all chosen for him as being the best to be illustrated, so that his training led him to grasp the central idea of the part of the book he desired to represent. At other times, and later, when the choice was left to himself, he almost always took the chief points, because they were the chief, and he never hesitated to undertake a scene because it was more difficult than some other passage easier to illustrate and close at hand. He chose the incident as being the best, and his teeming imagination did the rest.

The illustrations of Hablôt Browne are in all cases valuable additions to the interest and value of the book they embellish, and it is not too much to say that Lever and Ainsworth, and even Charles Dickens, were deeply indebted to his interpretation of their ideas for their early popularity. His plates have also in many cases saved volumes by lesser lights from total neglect, and given them a practical value their literary merits never would sustain.

Fac-simile of an address of a letter from Charles Dickens to " Phiz."

CHAPTER II.

THE ORIGINAL DRAWINGS FOR DICKENS'S WORKS.

THERE being an essential difference between the first sketches for many of the earlier illustrations by "Phiz" and the completed plates, I propose to say something about the original drawings for Dickens's works before treating of them in their published form.

As will be observed from the three designs of David Copperfield and his aunt which illustrate the previous chapter, there are occasionally very great changes made between the scene as it at first suggested itself to the artist and that finally adopted by him. The method "Phiz" followed, when engaged in preparing the sketches, was the necessary and very natural one of obtaining in the first place as much information as possible about the incident, and forming his designs accordingly. Not that he was always most successful when he had the best opportunity of studying the scene, for, as Dickens said, "Phiz" often did better work "without the text than with it;" and certainly he seemed to make more excellent illustrations when he had only a general description of what was required than when he had received an exact quotation. And this was the case up to the end. For the last

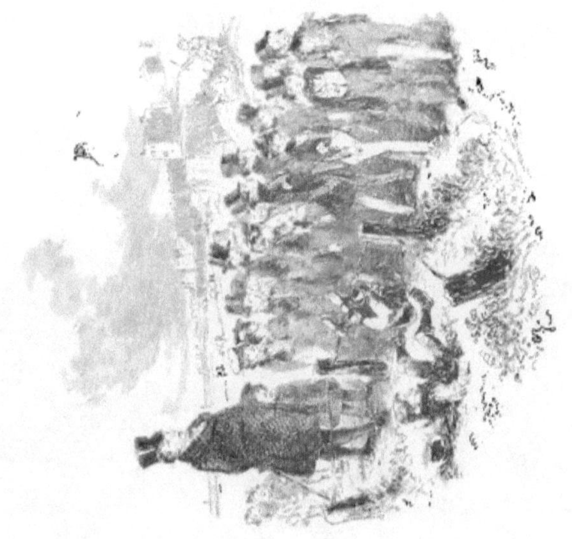

illustration "Phiz" drew (reproduced in this volume) Mr. Halse gave a general description of what he wanted, his experience being similar to Dickens's.

As I have said, it is not to be expected that "Phiz" is always thoroughly successful, even at his best time. Occasionally he executed the plate under disadvantage. For instance, when author and artist lived near each other, Dickens would sometimes drop in and read a portion of the novel he was writing, telling the artist that he desired the illustration taken from certain passages, and the whole scene would then be considered and thought out; but at other times, when under extreme pressure, Dickens would stay only a very few minutes, read what was to be illustrated, and run back to his writing-table without chatting over the points to be brought out particularly. In the latter case it would of course not be very surprising if some discrepancy existed between the letterpress and the plate.

At other times, however, Dickens would write out lengthy notes, partly literal extracts from the text and partly condensation. The following memorandum (kindly lent by Mr. Young) is an example of one of many that Dickens sent to "Phiz" when his illustrations were being prepared. It is specially interesting as throwing light on a point which has often been alluded to—that the description of Dr. Blimber and his "ten young gentlemen" does not agree with the seventeen youths presented in the etching. The illustration is printed here from the original plate, so that it may be compared with Dickens's directions to "Phiz."

"Paul (a year older) has left Mrs. Pipchin's, and gone to Doctor Blimber's establishment at Brighton. The Doctor only takes ten young gentlemen. Doctor Blimber's establishment is a great hothouse for the young mind, with a forcing apparatus always at work. Mental green peas are produced there at Christmas, and intellectual asparagus all the year round. Every description of Greek and Latin vegetable is got off the driest twigs of boys under the frostiest circumstances. Mrs. Blimber is fond of the boys not being like boys, and of their wearing collars and neckerchiefs. They have all blown before their time. The eldest boy in the school—young Toots by name, with a swollen nose and an exceedingly large head—left off blowing suddenly one day, and people *do* say that the Doctor rather overdid it with him, and that when he began to have whiskers he left off having brains. All the young gentlemen have great weights on their minds. They are haunted by verbs, noun-substantives, roots, and syntactic passages. Some abandoned hope half through the Latin Grammar, and others curse Virgil in the bitterness of their souls. Classical Literature in general is an immense collection of words to them. It's all words and grammar, and don't mean anything else.

"Subject. These young gentlemen, out walking, very dismally and formally (observe it's a very expensive school), with the lettering, *Doctor Blimber's young gentlemen as they appeared when enjoying themselves*. I think Doctor Blimber, a little removed from the rest, should bring up the rear, or lead the van, with Paul, who is much the youngest of the party. I extract the description of the Doctor (extract from Chapter XI., p. 73).

"Paul as last described, but a twelvemonth older. No collar or neckerchief for him, of course. I would make the next youngest boy about three or four years older than he."

I need not attempt to justify " Phiz " in his error respecting the number of " young gentlemen " introduced. We all know the story of the Academy student who in his careful attention to parts forgot the whole so far as to give six toes to a statue. But I would point out how successfully the artist has conveyed the impression of the boys being so very much " young gentlemen " by contrasting them with the urchins amusing themselves on the railings. These ragamuffins have enough of that which makes the whole world kin to see that the Greek and Latin vegetables would gladly throw off their intellectual asparagus to join in the sport of turning a somersault. So they eye the " young gentlemen " with a contempt which tells plainly that with all their poverty they have no wish to have their station altered, especially if it were to be changed to the unnatural discipline of good Doctor Blimber and his establishment.

It is worthy of mention that though such mistakes as in the Blimber plate did happen, Dickens was generally much pleased with the earlier work of " Phiz."* The artist worked hard and exerted all his powers in order to keep

* Most of the plates etched by " Phiz " were done on quarto steels; that is to say, two full-page illustrations on one plate, and thus it is sometimes necessary to introduce another subject a little irrelevantly. Florence busy with " Paul's exercise " is one of these, and is thus described:—" Many a night when they were all in bed, and when Miss Nipper, with her hair in papers and herself asleep in some uncomfortable attitude, reposed unconsciously by her side;"

up with the rapidly extending reputation of the writer; and we may now listen to what Dickens said in praise of another of the Dombey plates, and at the same time how he carefully suggested alterations in certain parts. This letter —which is also the property of Mr. Young—was sent to Furnival's Inn, the address being given in fac-simile of Dickens's writing in the headpiece to this chapter. A previous letter giving minute directions respecting this subject is printed at page 68.

"1, CHESTER PLACE, *Monday night, fifteenth March,* 1847.

"MY DEAR BROWNE,—The sketch is admirable; the women *quite perfect.* I cannot tell you how much I like the younger one. There are one or two points, however, which I must ask you to alter. They are capital in themselves, and I speak solely for the story.

"First—I grieve to write it—that Native, who is prodigiously good as he is, must be in European costume. He may wear earrings and look outlandish, and be dark brown. In this fashion he must be of Moses, Mosesy. I don't mean Old Testament Moses, but him of the Minories.

"Secondly, if you *can* make the Major older, and with a larger face, do.

"That's all. Never mind the Pump-room now, unless you have found the sketch, as we may have that another time. I shall propose to you a trip to Leamington together. We might go one day and return the next."

We have further evidence in this letter that it was Browne's habit to send the sketch to Dickens before he commenced his plate, and many of the original drawings are folded into a size easily carried through the post. The letter from Dickens, quoted a little later (p. 68), indicates that occasionally there was not time for this to be done, and when the rush of publication time came and the illustrations were not ready, it can easily be believed there was little time for delay, even for the important end of allowing the author to see that the text and drawing agreed.

Other authors were not so careful as Dickens in asking to inspect the drawings. Lever was almost always abroad, and never took the trouble. About Ainsworth there is no distinct record. But in one instance of a cut for

and when the chinking ashes in the grate were cold and grey; and when the candles were burnt down and guttering out;—Florence tried so hard to be a substitute for one small Dombey, that her fortitude and perseverance might have almost won her a free right to bear the name herself."

a Bulwer Lytton novel, a letter exists which shows that the illustration was done to the author's description, a proof was pulled, and then Lytton went over his text carefully to be sure that the two agreed.

 GREAT number of the original sketches that Phiz drew for the Dickens plates can be traced to owners at the present time, and these I have in every case carefully inspected and compared with the published illustrations.

Mr. Frederick Chapman, of the firm of Dickens's publishers (Messrs. Chapman and Hall) possesses a considerable number of the best drawings. He has the original designs for "Pickwick" and "Martin Chuzzlewit." Of the first, those of Seymour are as interesting as those by "Phiz," because of the attraction of their author's tragic end, and this more particularly with the "Dying Clown"—represented in facsimile in our Plate—which is noticed with the other "Pickwick" illustrations in Chapter III.

It is impossible to note all the changes introduced by "Phiz" into the plate, as compared with the first sketches. He treated the drawing more as a preliminary notion, and he appears never to have slavishly copied the drawing in all its detail on the plate, while in many cases he has made minor alterations. Some of the earlier Dickens drawings have written observations by the novelist, which in all cases are interesting, and occasionally throw a new light on the author's views. The next chapter refers to the "Pickwick" drawings, many of which have notes written on them. In the "Martin Chuzzlewit" sketches there are not many differences between them and the plate, but in the first two some alterations are made, this possibly arising from the difficulty the illustrator had in hitting at first the author's meaning. In the sketch of "The Meekness of Pecksniff," the figure of Tom Pinch is rubbed in hurriedly in pencil, the first idea having been evidently not to show him in the illustration. In a second drawing this figure is introduced carefully,

and, as in the Plate, is represented as just entering the room. For "Martin Chuzzlewit suspects Landlady," two drawings were also executed, but the second was probably only to guide the biter-in of the steel, so that the proper light and shade might be given. Sometimes when "Phiz" had not time to see the assistant who managed the acid work, he would send a rough indication just to help him to keep the chiaroscuro correct. The frontispiece with Tom Pinch was done very carefully in pencil by "Phiz," and a reproduction of it is here given. It is almost identical in conception with the plate, except the little figure of the footman behind the cigar. As remarked in connection with the reproduction of other drawings in this book, it forms an interesting study to compare it with the etching, which, of course, is reversed in printing.

Another owner of a large number of the original sketches is her Grace the Duchess of St. Albans, who has very courteously granted me permission to inspect and select from her collection. Her Grace possesses some of the finest specimens of Browne's Art, and I am happy to publish several in fac-simile from the Duchess's collection, which includes the "Dombey," "Bleak House," and the splendid "David Copperfield" drawings. It is not easy to decide which forms the best series: but on the whole I think the palm must be given to the premier sketches for "David Copperfield." They are very carefully executed, and differ from other sets of drawings by being nearly all highly finished. As the novel is the one Dickens himself liked best, it being so nearly his own story, so "Phiz" deemed it the most worthy of his greatest effort, and the splendid series of forty illustrations (in plates or in drawings) is unsurpassed. Some of the characters are, perhaps, not so successful as others—Agnes, for instance, realising little of the heroine described in the text; but David himself, especially when a boy, is most delightfully conceived. In a little note (now belonging to Mr. F. W. Cosens) Dickens wrote to "Phiz," asking to have a small alteration made in one of the "Copperfield" illustrations. He dates from Devonshire Terrace, Wednesday, ninth May, 1849 :—

H

"MY DEAR BROWNE,—I think the enclosed capital. Will you put Davy on a little jacket instead of this coat, without altering him in any other respect?—Faithfully ever, C. D."

This, I believe, refers to the drawing of the " Friendly Waiter." In the sketch in the Duchess of St. Albans' collection the coat of little David has been altered, and in the plate he wears a little jacket, as Dickens required.

The " Copperfield " drawings throughout are in fine condition. There is very little rubbed work, and only in a few instances have changes been made between the stages of drawing and etching.

The thirty-nine drawings of " Dombey," also the property of the Duchess of St. Albans, are not so carefully executed as the " Copperfield " designs, and yet they are not so rough in outline as those for " Bleak House." Some are in chalk, others in pencil alone, and a few have a mark of colour. A number also show marks of a red tinge, which arises from the fact that it was a red chalk tracing-paper " Phiz " employed when transferring the drawings to the steel, and the red has become mixed very slightly with the pencil.

The illustration, " Major Bagstock is delighted to have that opportunity," called forth a most interesting letter from Dickens to " Phiz," lent for publication here by Mr. Young, and printed for the first time. It thoroughly explains the plate :—

"1, CHESTER PLACE, REGENT'S PARK, *tenth March*, 1847.

"MY DEAR BROWNE,—I can't get into my own house, having come home before my time; and am living here until my Devonshire Terrace tenant performs that perfectly unintelligible ceremony, which is called in the vulgar, 'walking his chalks.'

"The occasion of my coming home makes me very late with my number, which I have only begun this morning; otherwise you should have been 'fed' sooner. My eldest boy's illness will excuse me I hope.

"The first subject I am now going to give is very important to the book. *I should like to see your sketch of it, if possible.*

"I should premise that I want to make the Major, who is the incarnation of selfishness and small revenge, a kind of comic Mephistophilean power in the book; and the No. begins with the departure of Mr. Dombey and the Major on that trip for change of air and scene which is prepared for in the last Number. They go to

Leamington, where you and I were once. In the Library the Major introduces Mr. Dombey to a certain lady, whom, as I wish to foreshadow dimly, said Dombey may come to marry in due season. She is about thirty, not a day more—handsome, though haughty looking—good figure, well dressed, showy, and desirable. Quite a lady in appearance, with something of a proud indifference about her, suggestive of a spark of the Devil within. Was married young. Husband dead. Goes about with an old mother, who rouges, and who lives upon the reputation of a diamond necklace and her family. Wants a husband. Flies at none but high game, and couldn't marry anybody not rich. Mother affects cordiality and heart, and is the essence of sordid calculation. Mother usually shoved about in a Bath chair by a page who has rather outgrown and outshoved his strength, and who butts at it behind like a ram, while his mistress steers herself languidly by a handle in front. Nothing the matter with her to prevent her walking, only was once when a Beauty sketched reclining in a Barouche, and having outlived the Beauty and the Barouche too, still holds to the attitude as becoming her uncommonly. Mother is in this machine in the sketch. Daughter has a parasol.

"The Major presents them to Mr. Dombey, gloating within himself over what may come of it, and over the discomfiture of Miss Tox. Mr. Dombey (in deep mourning) bows solemnly. Daughter bends. The native in attendance, bearing a camp-stool and the Major's greatcoat. Native evidently afraid of the Major and his thick cane. If you like it better, the scene may be in the street or in a green lane. But a great deal will come of it ; and I want the Major to express that, as much as possible in his apoplectic Mephistophilean observation of the scene, and in his share in it.

"Lettering, *Major Bagstock is delighted to have that opportunity.*"

The letter quoted a few pages earlier (page 65) has reference to the same plate, and is dated only five days later—after "Phiz" had sent the drawing, as requested in the tenth of March communication. The two form an interesting account of the growth of the illustration.

The design being, like many others, etched on a quarto steel, we have along with it the illustration of "Mr. Toots becomes particular—Diogenes also " :—

"'Perhaps you'd like to walk upstairs, Sir?' said Susan.

"'Well, I think I will come in !' said Mr. Toots.

"But instead of walking upstairs, the bold Toots made an awkward plunge at Susan, when the door was shut, and embracing that fair creature, kissed her on the cheek.

"'Go along with you!' cried Susan, 'or I'll tear your eyes out!'

"'Just another!' said Mr. Toots.

"'Go along with you!' exclaimed Susan, giving him a push. 'Innocents like you, too! Who'll begin next? Go along, Sir!'

"Susan was not in any serious strait, for she could hardly speak for laughing; but Diogenes, on the staircase, hearing a rustling against the wall, and a shuffling of feet, and seeing through the banisters that there was contention going on, and foreign invasion in the house, formed a different opinion, dashed down to the rescue, and in the twinkling of an eye had Mr. Toots by the leg.

"Susan screamed, laughed, opened the street-door, and ran down-stairs; the bold Toots tumbled staggering out into the street, with Diogenes holding on to one leg of his pantaloons, as if Burgess & Co. were his cooks, and had provided that dainty morsel for his holiday entertainment."

The forty drawings of "Bleak House" vary considerably in style. Several are very carefully drawn, being treated in the same masterly way as "My large order at the Bar" of "David Copperfield," and "My uncle Mobberly's Will" of "Mervyn Clitheroe." Others are rather loose—for instance, the "Spontaneous Combustion" plate, "The Appointed Time," is very sketchy. "The Mausoleum at Chesney Wold" and "Consecrated Ground"—Jo pointing out the grave—and one or two others, are merely rubbed in with crayons and colour mixed. The effects are obtained by the means that came readiest to the artist's hand, and not by any one method. The "Guppy" sketches are all capital, and the one where he enters the apartments of the Dedlocks, "A young man of the name of Guppy," is exceptionally clever.

The "Nicholas Nickleby" drawings are scattered, as the whole series of sketches were sold at Messrs. Robinson and Fisher's, in Old Bond Street, on July 16th, 1880. The thirty-eight drawings sold then realised £104 4s. 6d., being an average of nearly £2 15s. each. Some, however, went above this sum. The sketch, "Nicholas attracted by hearing his Sister's name mentioned," having some pencil remarks on it, was sold to Mr. Murray for £10 10s., and the same gentleman bought "Ralph Nickleby's Honest Composure" for £4 8s. Mr. Harvey bought "Great excitement of Miss

Kenwigs at the hairdresser's shop" for £8, and "Nicholas congratulating
Arthur Gride" for the same sum; both of these subjects are printed here.
Mr. Harvey also purchased the sketch of the "Mysterious appearance of the
man in small-clothes" for £3 5s. The other chief buyers at the sale were
Mr. Gall, Mr. Daniels, and Mr. Venables.

Mr. M. Speilman acquired, through Messrs. Robson and Kerslake, two
drawings, one of Squeers finding
Smike, entitled "A sudden recognition, unexpected on both sides," and
"The Recognition." The former
is specially interesting for having
a remark by Dickens written on it.
This note is partly cut away, but it
is to the effect that "I don't think
Smike is frightened enough," and
that Squeers is hardly "earnest
enough for my purpose," a hint
only partly taken by the illustrator,
as these defects are still visible in
the plate.

Mr. F. W. Cosens possesses
several preliminary sketches of the
Kenwigs children, one of which is
here reproduced in fac-simile.

Mr. Cosens also has an interest-
ing note from Dickens on the illustration of "Miss Kenwigs and Lillyvick in
the barber's." It is an instruction from the author to "Phiz." Dickens says
that the illustration is to be—

"A hairdresser's shop at night—not a dashing one, but a barber's. Morleena
Kenwig on a tall chair having her hair dressed by an underbred attendant with

his hair parted down the middle, and frizzed up into curls at the sides. Another customer, who is being shaved, has just turned his head in the direction of Miss Kenwigs, and she and Newman Noggs (who has brought her there, and has been whiling away the time with an old newspaper), recognise, with manifestations of surprise, and Morleena with emotion, Mr. Lillyvick, the collector. Mr. Lillyvick's bristly beard expresses great neglect of his person, and he looks very grim and in the utmost despondency."

This has been cleverly interpreted by "Phiz," as shown in the accompanying plate, and Dickens's condensation is interesting to read beside the text in the novel :—

"The old gentleman who had just been lathered, and who was sitting in a melancholy manner, with his face turned towards the wall, appeared quite unconscious of this incident, and to be insensible to everything around him, in the depth of reverie—a very mournful one, to judge from the sighs he occasionally vented—in which he was absorbed. Affected by this example, the proprietor began to clip Miss Kenwigs, the journeyman to scrape the old gentleman, and Newman Noggs to read last Sunday's paper — all three in silence : when Miss Kenwigs uttered a shrill little scream, and Newman, raising his eyes, saw that it had been elicited by the circumstance of the old gentleman turning his head, and disclosing the features of Mr. Lillyvick, the collector."

    *   *   *   *   *   *   *

"There he sat, with the remains of a beard at least a week old encumbering his chin ; a soiled and crumpled shirt-frill crouching, as it were, upon his breast, instead of standing out ; a demeanour so abashed and drooping, so despondent, expressive of such humiliation, grief, and shame, that if the souls of forty unsubstantial housekeepers, all of whom had had their water cut off for non-payment of the rate, could have been concentrated in one body, that one body could hardly have expressed such mortification and defeat as were now expressed in the person of Mr. Lillyvick, the collector.

"Newman Noggs uttered his name, and Mr. Lillyvick groaned, then coughed to hide it. But the groan was a full-sized groan, and the cough was but a wheeze.

" 'Is anything the matter?' said Newman Noggs.

" 'Matter, Sir!' cried Mr. Lillyvick, 'The plug of life is dry, Sir, and but the mud is left.'

"This speech, the style of which Newman attributed to Mr. Lillyvick's recent association with theatrical characters, not being quite explanatory, Newman looked as if he were about to ask another question, when Mr. Lillyvick prevented him by shaking his hand mournfully, and then waving his own.

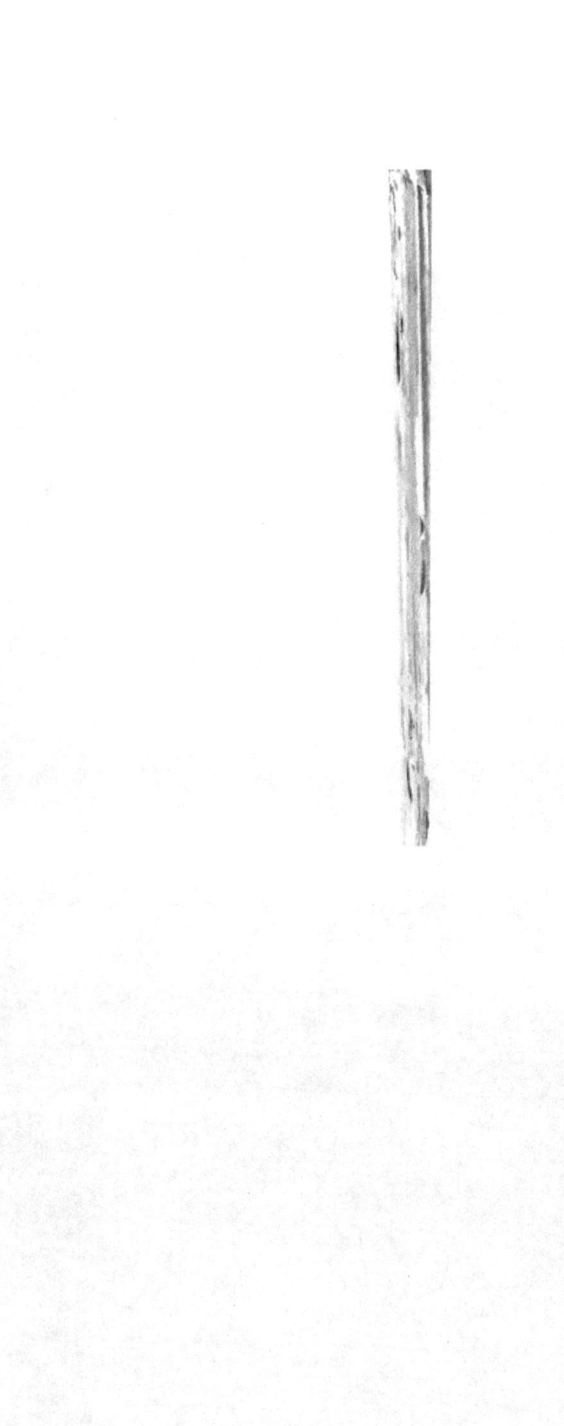

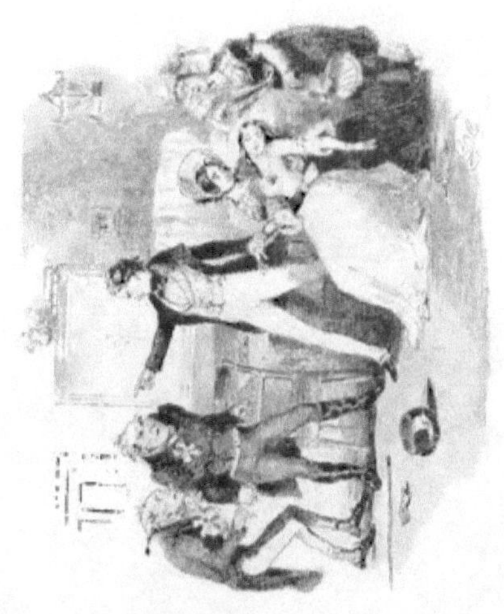

" ' Let me be shaved,' said Mr. Lillyvick, ' I shall be done before Morleena—it *is* Morleena, isn't it ?'

" ' Yes,' said Newman.

" ' Kenwigses have got a boy, haven't they ?' inquired the collector.

" Again Newman said ' Yes.'

" ' Is it a nice boy ?' demanded the collector.

" ' It ain't a very nasty one,' returned Newman, rather embarrassed by the question.

" ' Susan Kenwigs used to say,' observed the collector, ' that if ever she had another boy, she hoped it might be like me. Is this one like me, Mr. Noggs ?'

" This was a puzzling inquiry, but Newman evaded it by replying to Mr. Lillyvick that he thought the baby might possibly come like him in time.

" ' I should be glad to have somebody like me, somehow,' said Mr. Lillyvick, ' before I die.'

" ' You don't mean to do that yet awhile ?' said Newman.

" Unto which Mr. Lillyvick replied, in a solemn voice, ' Let me be shaved,' and again consigning himself to the hands of the journeyman, said no more."

The other illustration in the quarto plate, " Nicholas congratulates Arthur Gride on his wedding morning," is thus described in the volume :—

" Ralph Nickleby and Gride, stunned and paralysed by the awful event which had so suddenly overthrown their schemes (it would not otherwise, perhaps, have made much impression on them), and carried away by the extraordinary energy and precipitation of Nicholas, which bore down all before him, looked on at the proceedings like men in a dream or trance. It was not until every preparation was made for Madeline's immediate removal that Ralph broke silence by declaring she should not be taken away.

" ' Who says that ?' cried Nicholas, starting from his knee and confronting them, but still retaining Madeline's lifeless hand in his.

" ' I !' answered Ralph, hoarsely.

" ' Hush ! hush !' cried the terrified Gride, catching him by the arm again. ' Hear what he says.'

" ' Aye !' said Nicholas, extending his disengaged hand in the air, ' hear what he says. That both your debts are paid in one great debt of nature ; that the bond due to-day at twelve is now waste paper ; that your contemplated fraud shall be discovered yet ; that your schemes are known to man and overthrown by heaven ; wretches, that he defies you both to do your worst.'

" ' This man,' said Ralph, in a voice scarcely intelligible, ' this man claims his wife, and he shall have her.'

"'That man claims what is not his, and he should not have her if he were fifty men, with fifty more to back him,' said Nicholas.

"'Who shall prevent him?'

"'I will.'

"'By what right, I should like to know?' said Ralph. 'By what right, I ask?'

"'By this right—that, knowing what I do, you dare not tempt me further,' said Nicholas; 'and by this better right—that those I serve, and with whom you would have done me base wrong and injury, are her nearest and her dearest friends. In their name I bear her hence. Give way!'"

Mr. F. W. Cosens, of Melbury Road, Kensington, possesses a unique series of coloured drawings by "Phiz," illustrating "Pickwick," "David Copperfield," "Dombey," "Nicholas Nickleby," "Bleak House," and "Little Dorrit." These were commenced early in 1866, and completed in about three years. Mr. Cosens, a liberal patron of the Arts, hearing of Hablôt Browne's difficulties, called on him with the intention of making purchases; but finding that "Phiz" had little or nothing of the kind he wanted, Mr. Cosens commissioned the artist to make this series of coloured illustrations to Dickens's works. "Phiz" was rather in need of the money at the time, and the bargain was soon concluded. The artist, however, had not copies of Dickens's works, so he borrowed Mr. Cosens's books, and from these the drawings were made; they were probably traced and then tinted afterwards. Each of the volumes of drawings thus executed is accompanied by a written guarantee from "Phiz" that these are the only coloured illus-trations existing. A fac-simile is given here of the one in the "Pickwick" volume, which represents the artist sketching Pickwick; Sam Weller stands behind, and the figure of Apollo is put in as a contrast to Mr. Pickwick's portly figure.

As in all large series of drawings, these coloured illustrations vary much in value. "Phiz" has not troubled himself with inventing anything new. With one exception, the designs are simply replicas of the plates. The lines bear evidence of the tracing, having little of that mobility which an original

drawing invariably shows. The colouring is only now and again successful ;
though being slight, the delicacy of the tints takes away from the crudeness
that the same colour laid on more deeply would have had. Generally
the colouring is pleasing, and now and then some strong pieces of good
colour are shown; not in the figures, but in the landscape or architectural
backgrounds.

Old Weller and his Grandson.   From "Master Humphrey's Clock."

CHAPTER III.

THE ILLUSTRATIONS TO "PICKWICK," DRAWINGS AND PLATES.

HERE being more variety in the "Pickwick" plates than in any other of the books illustrated by "Phiz," I devote a chapter specially to the consideration of the volume. It is one that every admirer of Dickens and "Phiz" desires to possess, and there being many differences in the plates, it is a matter of some moment also to the bibliographer to have these varieties clearly set forth.

The method of Hablôt Browne's etching being described in another chapter, it is only necessary to say here that the illustrator, who first called himself "Nemo," then "Phiz," followed the procedure of Seymour, his predecessor, and used steel plates for his etchings. These were etched with the graver by Browne, and then bitten up with acid by an assistant.

In the original edition, published in one shilling monthly parts from the beginning of 1836 to the end of 1837, the first seven illustrations are by Robert Seymour, the next two are by R. W. Buss, and the remaining thirty-four by Hablôt Browne. Of the latter, the first two (that is the tenth and eleventh plates) are signed "Nemo," but in the twelfth this is changed to "Phiz," and so continues to the end. Each plate is double the size of the page, and holds two subjects side by side, there being thus twenty-one plates besides one single plate of "The Dying Clown," by Seymour. The two Buss plates being bad productions, were cancelled, and "Phiz" etched other two to take their places; one of the subjects not being repeated, "The Influence of the Salmon" replacing "The Cricket-Field." Copies with the Buss plates are now rare, there having been only about seven hundred published; but it must not be imagined that volumes which do not contain these Buss plates are much inferior to others which have the "Phiz." As a rule they are less excellent, but this is not necessarily so, for reasons to be presently explained.

The plates were all some time later, except the two which replaced the Buss plates, etched in duplicate, the first by Seymour being re-drawn and etched by Hablôt Browne. This was necessary on account of the large sale, which required more impressions than one plate could give without serious deterioration: a plan of duplication which was pursued in the more popular of the succeeding novels, as detailed in the succeeding chapter.

The duplicate plates of "Pickwick" appear to have commenced at the date of the publication of Part 10 (end of 1836); for up to that number we find all the parts contain either impressions of the first set of plates or of the second; but after Part 10 impressions from the first and second plates are mixed indiscriminately. The evidence of sameness of style of workmanship shows that after this part the second plates, though varying a little in detail, have the same character as the first; but the second series of the twenty earliest plates shows considerable advance in manner over those done at the date of first publication.

The reason for this appears to be that it was not until Part 10 was issued that the plan of duplication was hit on, and that when it was the previous parts were reprinted entirely from the newer plates, thus making the parts to number 10 contain either impressions from the first series or the second without intermixture. But after Part 10, the plates being printed at the same time, the impressions were sent to the binder together, and it frequently happened that impressions from either plate were bound up in one part. As explained, the steels are quarto size, and each holds two subjects; an impression from the duplicate plates would give four illustrations, which we will call A 1 and A 2, and B 1 and B 2; the binder often took A 1 and B 2, or A 2 and B 1, to put in the part, thus giving the illustrations rightly enough, but mixing the series and puzzling the collector greatly.

For these reasons it may safely be affirmed that there are very few perfect volumes of "Pickwick" existing with every illustration from the first plates throughout. A certain collector has four copies of the work in the parts, with the original covers, advertisements, &c., but not one on examination can be found to have the first states entirely, though, by careful exchanging, one perfect volume with first state illustrations has been made up, but this only after great labour.*

When Messrs. Chapman and Hall projected the publication, it was arranged that each number of the "Pickwick Papers" should contain twenty-four pages of letterpress and four illustrations on steel. For one shilling this was too large to be commercially successful. To-day no publisher would be venturesome enough to promise so much for a work whose merit had yet to be tested; and even for a book that would reach the sale that Dickens's did, four plates in each shilling part overweighted the publication.

* It may also be worthy of note that "Pickwick," when in two volumes, has only a title-page added, marked "Volume II.," which begins without preliminary at Chapter XXIX.

The cost of the first number made this apparent to the publishers, and they at once began to consider the question of reducing the number of plates and making up the difference to purchasers by adding eight pages to the letterpress. Seymour's suicide* immediately after the first part had appeared left the publishers little choice in the matter; three only of the plates for Part 2 were then completed, and there was not time enough to obtain another. Therefore it was decided that in the future each part should consist of thirty-two pages of text, with only two etchings. This was a sounder arrangement for the publishers, and one that was found to work well for many years to come.

In the preface to the first edition, Dickens alludes to " Phiz " in a slightly apologetic strain, doubtless occasioned by a twitch of conscience at the difficulties into which his own procrastination threw the artist. " It is due to the gentleman whose designs accompany the letterpress to state that the interval has been so short between the production of each number in manu-script and its appearance in print, that the greater portion of the illustrations have been executed by the artist from the author's mere verbal description of what he intended to write."

How many etchers are there in England at the present time who would agree to work on the same terms? There are several clever draughtsmen who can incorporate an idea with a design quickly enough, and then hand it to an engraver to be cut in wood. But the ways of etchers on copper (as mostly employed now) or on steel, as " Phiz " used, are different from what they were fifty years ago.

" Phiz " would, when hard pressed, etch a plate in one day, have it bitten in by a friend in the evening, and ready for the printer the succeeding day. Of course, the mere manual labour in most modern etching would make this impossible to be done; publishers will not be content with the free work " Phiz " was compelled to execute, and they pay for laboured detail, while much of the *verve* and genius slips from their illustrations.

* Robert Seymour committed suicide by shooting himself in the head, on April 20th, 1836.

It is impossible to say, and useless to speculate, what reputation " Phiz"
would have obtained had Robert Seymour lived.   Seymour's designs display
an equal knowledge of composition and draughtsmanship, and though they
lack the rollicking humour of " Phiz," they faithfully adhere to the story.
Seymour's original sketches are thin compared with Hablôt Browne's.   They
are in hard outline and tinted with sepia, as shown in our fac-simile of
the drawing of " The Dying Clown," and are not nearly so complete in
details as in the finished etching on the plate.   It is also worth noting that
all Seymour's originals are drawn exactly as printed, showing that he
must have reversed his design as he drew on the steel.*   " The Dying
Clown" is a story introduced into " Pickwick," and ends in the following
way :—

"At the close of one of these paroxysms, when I had with great difficulty held
him down in his bed, he sank into what appeared to be a slumber. Overpowered
with watching and exertion, I had closed my eyes for a few minutes when I felt a
violent clutch on my shoulder. I awoke instantly. He had raised himself up so as
to seat himself in bed ; a dreadful change had come over his face, but consciousness
had returned, for he evidently knew me. The child, who had long since been
disturbed by his ravings, rose from its little bed and ran towards its father, screaming with fright. The mother hastily caught it in her arms, lest he should injure it
in the violence of his insanity ; but, terrified by the alteration of his features, stood
transfixed by the bedside. He grasped my shoulder convulsively, and, striking his
breast with the other hand, made a desperate attempt to articulate. It was unavailing ; he extended his arm towards them and made another violent effort. There
was a rattling noise in the throat, a glare of the eye, a short, stifled groan ; and he
fell back—dead!"

The two illustrations by R. W. Buss, "Cricket," and " The Fat Boy
discovering Tupman and Rachel," are sandwiched between the valuable
plates by Seymour and the clever designs by "Phiz."   It may frankly be
said of them, and that without unnecessary disparagement of their author's

* Although the temptation is great, I will not enter into the question whether Dickens or Seymour first
conceived the idea of Pickwick and his Club, but I may say all my investigations lead me to believe Dickens the
originator, in the best sense of the term, of the ever-fascinating story.

merits as a painter and lecturer, that they are painfully and unutterably bad.*
They are indeed almost without redeeming quality, the hands and heads
being especially feeble.   Though circumstances forced their publication to

Unpublished design by R. W. Buss, for " Pickwick."

the extent of several hundreds, they were withdrawn as soon as possible and
their places taken by two etched by " Phiz."   It is known to few that Buss

* The principal works in oil painting by R. W. Buss were " The Hearty Squeeze," " Satisfaction," " Frosty
Morning," " The First of September," " Soliciting a Vote," " Time and Tide wait for no Man," and " Christmas
in the Olden Time."   Buss also painted several actors—Macready, Buckstone, Reeve, Liston, Mrs. Nisbet, and
Miss Ellen Tree.   He contributed many woodcuts to Knight's editions of " London," " Chaucer," " Shakspere,"
and " Old England," and was one of the exhibitors in the Westminster Hall competition in 1843.   His lectures on
" Comic and Satiric Art," " Fresco," and " The Beautiful and Picturesque," were at one time well known in the
provinces.   He died in 1876.   His volume on " English Graphic Satire " (1874) is an excellent compilation, the
result of much laborious study.

executed another plate for "Pickwick," one which he submitted to the publishers, and from its comparative success gained the commission to take Seymour's place. Being extremely rare and unpublished, I have introduced a fac-simile of it for the sake of comparison. The incident is at page 35, when Pickwick is told to "keep back" at the grand review at Rochester.*

The first of Hablôt Knight Browne's illustrations, as regards position, is at page 89 of the original edition, and represents Mr. Wardle's coach breaking down in the chase after Jingle and Miss Rachel. But the first that "Phiz" etched was his creation of Sam Weller as he stands brushing boots in the old George Inn at Southwark :—

"Two plump gentlemen and one thin one entered the yard and looked round in search of some authorized person, of whom they could make a few inquiries. Mr. Samuel Weller happened to be at the moment engaged in burnishing a pair of painted tops, the personal property of a farmer who was refreshing himself with a slight lunch of two or three pounds of cold beef and a pot or two of porter, after the fatigues of the Borough Market; and to him the thin gentleman straightway advanced.

"'My friend,' said the thin gentleman.

"'You're one o' the adwice gratis order,' thought Sam, 'or you wouldn't be so wery fond o' me all at once.' But he only said, 'Well, sir.'

"'My friend,' said the thin gentleman, with a conciliatory hem, 'have you got many people stopping here now? Pretty busy, eh?'

"Sam stole a look at the inquirer. He was a little high-dried man, with a dark squeezed-up face, and small restless black eyes, that kept winking and twinkling on each side of his little inquisitive nose, as if they were playing a perpetual game of peep-bo with the features. He was dressed all in black, with boots as shiny as his eyes, a low white neckcloth, and a clean shirt with a frill to it; a gold watch-chain and seals depended from his fob. He carried his black kid gloves in his hands, not on them, and as he spoke thrust his wrists beneath his coat-tails with the air of a man who was in the habit of propounding some regular posers.

"'Pretty busy, eh?' said the little man.

* This plate has been reproduced in photo-lithography, and may sometimes be met with in this state in volumes. The two suppressed Buss plates—"Cricket" and "Tupman and Rachel," have also been copied in steel by a living etcher, but the copies, being printed on India paper, never can be mistaken for originals.

"'Oh, wery well, sir,' replied Sam, 'we shan't be bankrupts, and we shan't make our fort'ns. We eats our biled mutton without capers, and don't care for horseradish ven ve can get beef.'

"'Ah!' said the little man, 'you're a wag, a'nt you?'

"'My eldest brother was troubled with that complaint,' said Sam : 'it may be catching, I used to sleep with him.'

"'This is a curious old house of yours,' said the little man, looking round him.

"'If you'd sent word you was a-coming we'd ha' had it repaired,' replied the imperturbable Sam.

"The little man seemed rather baffled by these several repulses, and a short consultation took place between him and the two plump gentlemen."

Mr. Robert Young, Browne's early friend and assistant, has related to me his impressions of the circumstances under which this plate was executed.

When Hablôt Browne had left the service of Finden, the engraver, and was setting up as a draughtsman, he saw the two illustrations by Buss, and called at Chapman's with specimens of his work for Dickens to see. William Makepeace Thackeray was another artist who had similar thoughts, and he too submitted drawings for the author's inspection. As fortunately for the future author of "Vanity Fair" as for the future "Phiz," the choice fell on Hablôt Browne. Fortunate it was, because Thackeray never would have made a good illustrator; and fortunate was it for Browne, for without Dickens to illustrate his skill would never have gained him great fame, while associated with such stories, the artist was assured of an audience as wide as the use of the English language. Browne and Dickens also were already known to each other, for the little pamphlet "Sunday under three heads," written by the author of "Pickwick" under the *nom de plume* of Timothy Sparks, had been illustrated by H. K. B.

At this time Browne was lodging in Newman Street. He called one evening on Mr. Young at his rooms, then in Chester Place, Regent's Park, just after dinner. Mr. Young was still engaged with Finden, the line engraver (where Hablôt Browne had been apprenticed), and he had mastered all the technical work of biting-in a steel plate with acid after it had been

K

etched, this being a partly artistic and partly mechanical process which Browne never undertook to do himself. Browne on entering said, "Look here, old fellow: will you come to my rooms to assist me with a plate I have to etch?' On Mr. Young—being as obliging a man as ever lived—readily assenting to go, Browne told him to take his key with him, as they might be late. The result was that the two conspirators sat up all night working hard at the steel. Browne's work at etching the design was done before he called on Mr. Young, so that the biting-in was the occupation of the night, while both indulged in flights of fancy as to the final outcome of the good fortune that was then dawning on the young artist.

This was the illustration of "Sam Weller at the Inn," as just described, and the impressions in this volume are taken from the identical plate etched at this time. Mr. Young's part of the work consisted in rendering the lines etched with a needle on the steel by Browne the proper depth of colour by the application and manipulation of acid; and this without necessarily adding or taking away from the artistic merit of the production. The design (called in later editions, when titles were added to the plates, "The first appearance of Sam Weller,") is an inimitable composition, one in which Sam was created and Pickwick perpetuated, and which must have made Dickens's heart warm as he looked at it and became conscious that Seymour's place would certainly be more than filled by the young man who then signed himself "Nemo." It is not certainly so cleverly drawn as the second plate of the same subject done later; it is influenced by the study of Seymour's illustrations, and shows want of experience; but it went very far to make the success of the publication assured, was a distinct advance on Seymour's plates, and was not to be named in the same breath with Buss's productions. In the first plate, as will be observed, Mr. Wardle's "smalls" are dark-coloured and the dog beside Pickwick is black; in the second the dog is white, and Wardle's garments light-coloured; a Wellington boot also stands on the first step, which does not appear in the original plate.

The design on the other half of the plate, " The Breakdown," is equal in merit with the Sam Weller design, but it is not Hablôt Browne's unfettered work, exhibiting the same influences as the other. The incident is thus described :—

> " After a few seconds of bewilderment and confusion, in which nothing but the plunging of horses and breaking of glass, could be made out, Mr. Pickwick felt himself violently pulled out from among the ruins of the chaise ; and as soon as he had gained his feet and extricated his head from the skirts of his greatcoat, which materially impeded the usefulness of his spectacles, the full disaster of the case met his view.
>
> " Old Mr. Wardle, without a hat and his clothes torn in several places, stood by his side, and the fragments of the chaise lay scattered at their feet. The post-boys, who had succeeded in cutting the traces, were standing, disfigured with mud and disordered by hard riding, by the horses' heads. About a hundred yards in advance was the other chaise, which had pulled up on hearing the crash. The postillions, each with a broad grin convulsing his countenance, were viewing the adverse party from their saddles, and Mr. Jingle was contemplating the wreck from the coach window with evident satisfaction. The day was just breaking, and the whole scene was rendered perfectly visible by the grey light of the morning.
>
> " ' Hallo ! ' shouted the shameless Jingle, ' anybody damaged ?—elderly gentlemen—no light weights—dangerous work—very.'
>
> " ' You're a rascal ! ' roared Wardle.
>
> " ' Ha ! ha ! ' replied Jingle, and then he added, with a knowing wink and jerk of the thumb towards the interior of the chaise—'I say—she's very well—desires her compliments—begs you won't trouble yourself—love to Tuppy—won't you get up behind ?—drive on boys.'
>
> " The postillions resumed their proper attitudes ; away rattled the chaise, Mr. Jingle fluttering in derision a white handkerchief from the coach window."

The threatening attitude of Mr. Wardle is perhaps the cleverest point, though not the most readily seen ; and the figures at the distant chaise are hit off in a few touches of remarkable cleverness. The second version of this plate varies greatly from this : the upraised arm of Mr. Wardle is altered ; there are four horses seen ; no wheel is lying in the foreground ; the driver standing beside the horses is not the same man, and the carriage and foliage are treated in manner differing from the original.

T would be tiresome as well as unnecessary to go through the illustrations to note each one's quality; but there are a number which call for special consideration on account of changes between the original sketch and the published etching, and also because of differences in the two sets of plates used to illustrate " Pickwick." Besides these, a few of the drawings have remarks written on them by Dickens, and as they are in all cases interesting I give them *in extenso.*

The original sketch for " Mrs. Leo Hunter's Fancy Dress Déjeuné " represents the hostess of the house as old and inclined to *embonpoint.* This, with other minor details, not meeting with the author's entire approval, Dickens has written below the drawing, " I think it would be better if Pickwick had hold of [the] Bandit's arm. If Minerva [Mrs. Leo Hunter] *tried* to look a little younger (more like Mrs. Pott, who is perfect) I think it would be an additional improvement." The design, in the transferring to the steel, was accordingly altered by making Mrs. Leo Hunter thinner and with an evident affectation of youth. The Bandit's arm is not, however, taken hold of by Pickwick, whose position is slightly altered—and for the better—while some of the other figures vary a little.

In the illustration of the " First Interview with Mr. Sergeant Snubbin," the plate follows the sketch almost exactly. But in the drawing the Sergeant's face is rubbed out, and Dickens has written underneath, " I think the Sergeant should look younger and a great deal more sly and knowing ; he should be looking at Pickwick, too, smiling compassionately at his innocence. The other fellows are noble.—C. D." The face in the sketch is obliterated, but the plate shows that " Phiz " carried out Dickens's instructions.

Mr. Winkle's situation when the door " blew to " is repeated exactly on the plate, except that the candlestick is in his hand at its ordinary level in the drawing and being held overhead in the plate. Below the sketch in faint pencil "Phiz" has written, "Shall I leave Pickwick where he is or put him under the bedclothes. I can't carry him so high as the second floor.—II. K. B." Pickwick's lodgings being on the upper floor, he would naturally be expected to open a window there, but the novelist has, presumably, made the text to suit the illustration, and let him remain on the first floor. In reply, but not exactly in answer, Dickens writes on the drawing, "Winkle should be holding the candlestick above his head, I think. It looks more comical, the light having gone out. A *fat* chairman so short as our friend here never drew breath in Bath. I would leave him where he is decidedly. Is the lady full dressed: she ought to be.—C. D." As the novel speaks of the one chairman as short and fat and the other long and thin, and of the extinguished candle being held above Winkle's head all the time (as in the plate), it is probable that Dickens made such little changes in his text as would make the illustration agree.

It is also interesting to note that when "Phiz" sent the sketch of "Mr. Winkle returns under extraordinary circumstances" to Dickens, he wrote underneath to the author, "Dear Sir,—Will you be good enough to send the sketch on to Chapman and Hall when you have done with it.—H. K. B." In this drawing "Phiz" has not made Sam Weller and the housemaid quite to Dickens's liking, so the latter has written on the drawing, "Are Sam and the housemaid clearly made out, and [would it not be] better if he were looking on, with his arm round [Mary]. I rather question the accuracy of the housemaid." * At the foot of the sketch Browne has written instructions about the biting-in. "The outlines of the figures I have etched with a broad point unintentionally; bite them slightly, that they may not be too hard, especially Pickwick." The figures of Sam and Mary, though blurred in the drawing, fall into their places with proper clear-

* The words in brackets do not appear in the sketch, as it is cut close. I fill them in, in what appears to me the correct way.—D. C. T.

ness in the plate, and the whole is certainly better in the etching than in the
original sketch.

"PICKWICK" DRAWINGS FAC-SIMILIED.

The drawings by "Phiz" here reproduced in fac-simile have been chosen
because of the interest of the incident presented. There will be found but
few differences between them and the plates. In Mrs. Bardell fainting in
Pickwick's arms a minor variation will be found in the armchair at the
back: in the sketch it is open-backed, and in the etching covered all over.
The following is the portion of "Pickwick" which the drawing illustrates:—

"'Oh you kind, good, playful dear,' said Mrs. Bardell; and without more ado
she rose from her chair and flung her arms round Mr. Pickwick's neck, with a
cataract of tears and a chorus of sobs.

"'Bless my soul,' cried the astonished Mr. Pickwick; 'Mrs. Bardell, my good
woman—dear me, what a situation—pray consider—Mrs. Bardell, don't—if anybody
should come—'

"'Oh, let them come,' exclaimed Mrs. Bardell, frantically; 'I'll never leave you,
dear, kind, good soul;' and, with these words, Mrs. Bardell clung the tighter.

"'Mercy upon me,' said Mr. Pickwick, struggling violently, 'I hear somebody
coming up the stairs. Don't, don't, there's a good creature, don't.' But entreaty and
remonstrance were alike unavailing, for Mrs. Bardell had fainted in Mr. Pickwick's
arms, and before he could gain time to deposit her on a chair Master Bardell
entered the room, ushering in Mr. Tupman, Mr. Winkle, and Mr. Snodgrass.

"Mr. Pickwick was struck motionless and speechless. He stood with his lovely
burden in his arms, gazing vacantly on the countenances of his friends without the
slightest attempt at recognition or explanation. They, in their turn, stared at him;
and Master Bardell, in his turn, stared at everybody.

"The astonishment of the Pickwickians was so absorbing, and the perplexity of
Mr. Pickwick so extreme, that they might have remained in exactly the same
relative situations until the suspended animation of the lady was restored, had it
not been for a most beautiful and touching expression of filial affection on the part of
her youthful son. Clad in a tight suit of corduroy spangled with brass buttons of a
very considerable size, he at first stood at the door, astounded and uncertain; but,
by degrees, the impression that his mother must have suffered some personal damage
pervaded his partially developed mind, and considering Mr. Pickwick as the
aggressor, he set up an appalling and semi-earthly kind of howling, and, butting
forward with his head, commenced assailing that immortal gentleman about the

back and legs, with such blows and pinches as the strength of his arm and the violence of his excitement allowed.

"'Take this little villain away,' said the agonized Mr. Pickwick, 'he's mad.'

"'What *is* the matter,' said the three tonguetied Pickwickians.

"'I don't know,' replied Mr. Pickwick, pettishly. 'Take away the boy.' (Here Mr. Winkle carried the interesting boy, screaming and struggling, to the further end of the apartment.) 'Now help me, lead this woman down-stairs.'

"'Oh, I am better now,' said Mrs. Bardell, faintly.

"'Let me lead you down-stairs,' said the ever gallant Mr. Tupman.

"'Thank you, sir, thank you,' exclaimed Mrs. Bardell, hysterically. And downstairs she was led accordingly, accompanied by her affectionate son.

"'I cannot conceive what has been the matter with that woman. I had merely announced to her my intention of keeping a man-servant when she fell into the paroxysm in which you found her. Very extraordinary thing.'

"'Very,' said his three friends.

"'Placed me in such an extremely awkward situation,' continued Mr. Pickwick.

"'Very,' was the reply of his followers, as they cough slightly, and look dubiously at each other.

"This behaviour was not lost upon Mr. Pickwick. He remarked their incredulity. They evidently suspected him."

In "The Trial" scene more difference is visible between the original and the plate. The back of the seat where Pickwick sits has been reduced considerably in height, and the figures thereby brought more together. The drawing, it will be observed, places Perker's hat on the seat beside him, but only one of the plates has this. The alteration in the back of the front seat also makes some change necessary in Sergeant Buzfuz, and his papers are transferred to his other hand, the left; this, because of the usual reversing in etching, is the same hand in which they are held in the plate. A comparison of the fac-simile (over-leaf) is extremely interesting. The drawing illustrates :—

"Here Mr. Pickwick, who had been writhing in silence for some time, gave a violent start, as if some vague idea of assaulting Sergeant Buzfuz in the august presence of justice, of law, suggested itself to his mind. An admonitory gesture from Perker restrained him, and he listened to the learned gentleman's continuation with a look of indignation, which contrasted forcibly with the admiring faces of Mrs. Cluppins and Mrs. Sanders."

The changes in one or two of the others may be summarised together. The illustration, "Election at Eatanswill," is similar in general effect in plate and drawing, but the details vary almost throughout, many of the figures being in quite different attitudes. The "Christmas Eve at Mr. Wardle's" was drawn twice, once in pencil, and then in pencil washed with sepia, like most of the others. For "The Goblin and the Sexton" "Phiz" made no less than three drawings, which is an unique circumstance in the Dickens illustrations. The first follows but haltingly the description in the text: the goblin's tongue is not out, his hat is not broad-brimmed, nor are his legs crossed. In the second the result is better: the hat and legs are as described, but the tongue is not out. In the third the figure is exactly as described, and St. Albans church is introduced in the background very delicately and beautifully.

Two drawings were made for "The Warden's Room." The first is quite different from the text: the man in the etching singing a comic song with comparative tranquillity, is in the sketch kicking up his heels and behaving uproariously; Pickwick in the drawing is only waking, and not sitting up in bed, and Smangle is standing up, while in the plate he is seated. The second drawing is copied in the published illustration, and it is much the better composition of the two. In the sketch where "Job Trotter encounters Sam in Mr. Muggles's kitchen," Sam and the maid are differently treated: Sam has taken the girl on his knee, his arm around her, while the bashful maiden pretends to struggle to be let free. In the plate Mary is standing and Sam is on a different side of the table.

It may further be noted that in the Valentine drawing old Weller is without a hat, and the chair has not his greatcoat thrown over it; that in "Conviviality at Bob Sawyer's" there is a skeleton in the original beside the cupboard not in the plate; and that the countryman at the back, in "Bob Sawyer's Method of Travelling," is simply walking with bundle over shoulder in the drawing, while in the etching he is waving it.

Before considering the variations in the plates of the original edition, I
will now mention the other editions of Pickwick. In the cheap edition of 1857
the single illustration is "by C. R. Leslie, Esq., R.A." Leslie, as a painter
of something more than ordinary merit, would be placed by many people far
above Hablôt Browne in the scale of Art; yet here he quite fails to convey
the humour of the story, and in an attempt to be highly finished and

Mr. Pickwick and Mrs. Bardell. 1874.

academical with a subject better treated otherwise, he falls very far short
of "Phiz." Six extra illustrations to "Pickwick" on wood were afterwards
published separately by "Phiz," to make up for this abortive attempt at
illustration, and these are well worth having.

In 1874, "Phiz" again illustrated "Pickwick," for the Household Edition,
with fifty-eight new woodcuts. Many if not most of them follow the design

of the original edition, but very far behind them in merit. The best is
"Mrs. Bardell and Pickwick," of which an impression is here given to compare
with the first idea of the artist in the original sketch. The reproduction of
that sketch is not completely satisfactory, but it is sufficient to indicate the
gulf that lies between the Art of "Phiz" in 1837 and 1874.

VARIATIONS IN THE PLATES OF THE ORIGINAL EDITION.

The seven plates by Seymour for "Pickwick" were, like all the others,
executed in duplicate after the success of the book was certain, and they
were probably etched by Hablôt Browne at the time he did the second series
of his own, but on this point there is no evidence, although it is usually
taken for granted that such was the case. The variations in these seven
illustrations are not, however, of any artistic importance, the chief being in
"The Dying Clown," at page 31. In the first plate the listener's hat touches
his foot, in the second it is a little distance away; and there are some other
minor differences which with the help of the fac-simile in this volume can be
easily found. It is interesting to note also the change in the posture of the
listener between the sketch and the etching. "The Cricket Match"
appears in the first of the original editions only, the plate having been
suppressed and the design not repeated, as in "The Fat Boy awakes," which
was illustrated both by Buss and "Phiz." These Buss plates have disap-
peared, and the collector may be cautioned against the copies recently
published by certain dealers. The illustration to replace "The Cricket
Match" was "The Influence of the Salmon," used only after the suppression
of Buss's design. The "First Appearance of Sam Weller" is referred to at
page 88, "The Breakdown" at page 93, and "Mrs. Bardell fainting in
Mr. Pickwick's arms" at page 96. "The Eatanswill Election" varies
greatly in the two treatments of the subject; the general effect is similar,
but the mayor stands with his legs apart in the second plate, and in the
crowd underneath some of the figures are in different positions. A minute

variation is in the long hat behind Pickwick: in some copies it has a cockade, thus making the figure Sam Weller.

In the plate showing Pickwick behind the door of the young ladies' seminary, some of the earliest impressions have page 154 underneath instead of page 159, as it should be, and many of the later copies bear evidence of this number having been altered. The bell behind the door is only in the second plate.

"Mrs. Leo Hunter's Fancy Dress Déjeuné" is an illustration displaying great variations at a glance. In the first plate there is a pool in the foreground and a birdcage on the tree high up among the branches, and the great Pott is not unlike Lord Brougham. In the second the Brigand has a hat and feathers, with knees bent, and Pickwick extends both his arms. In "Pickwick and Sam in the Attorney's Office" Sam's legs in the first are together and in the second apart; and the first etching of "Pickwick in the Pound" has a young ass which does not appear in the second, and there are more youngsters in the second.

The two plates of the middle-aged lady in the double-bedded room have quite different figures. In the second she is plumper and younger, and her dress over the chair is light, while in the first it is dark. "Christmas Eve at Mr. Wardle's" in the first had a cat and dog in the front, which are neither in the original drawing nor in the second plate. In "The Goblin and the Sexton" there is a bone beside the skull in one plate, not in the other. "The Valentine" differs in having a newspaper on the ground in the second plate which is not in the first; and in the trial scene Perker's hat is on a seat in one and is absent in the other, as already noticed in connection with the sketches.

Such are some of the chief variations in the Pickwick plates. None of the other Dickens books have so long a story, and it will be observed that it is in the earlier plates that the principal variations lie. This was because as "Phiz" settled down to work he hit the right subject, and carried it out more easily than, naturally, he could do at first.

Comparing the "Pickwick" plates with later illustrations to Dickens, it must
be admitted that they are not so fine as those done in subsequent years, and
a distinct advance can even be traced as the plates go on.　　The early work
reveals some need of experience in the technical difficulties of the art, and in
several instances the drawing and composition are improved in the second
plate of the same subject, notably in "The Breakdown," which is not so good
in the original plate as in the duplicate.　　On the whole, however, "Pickwick"
may be taken as a typical example of the earlier art of Hablôt Browne, and
the valuable place it holds in the connoisseur's eyes is as much because of his
delightful designs as of the interest attached to the story of the illustrations.

Barnaby Rudge and the Raven.　　From "Master Humphrey's Clock."

Mrs. Jarley and Nell. From an unpublished block for " The Old Curiosity Shop," in " Master Humphrey's Clock."

CHAPTER IV.

THE ILLUSTRATIONS FOR DICKENS'S WORKS OTHER THAN " PICKWICK."

FTER the experience gained in the preparation of the " Pick-wick " illustrations, " Phiz " worked more smoothly, and made his duplicate plates so very nearly alike that it is not necessary to point out the variations, as has been done for the first large work he illustrated. It is further unne-cessary to do this because—let dealers and collectors say what they will—there is now no way of telling which plate of any subject was really etched first, as the two, three, or four plates of the one illustration were all executed at the same time. There are indeed "first states" of the plates, but no first or second editions, as in "Pickwick," and early impressions can only be told by examination of each individual volume. No precise guide can be given, further than the recommendation to the collector to use all the knowledge he possesses of etchings in general to enable him to arrive at a satisfactory conclusion as to whether the impressions are worn or not. This is a knowledge that only comes by long experience, though it may be said generally that when the illustration is rich in colour and full of perceptible detail, with the innumerable half-tints so dear to the artist, not having sudden transitions from dull black to meaningless white, the collector may fairly and safely conclude that the impressions are "early."

Following our experience with the "Pickwick" illustrations, we find in all the other volumes of Dickens's works illustrated by Hablôt Browne that the earlier ones are the most interesting and have more to be said about their plates than the later; and that next to "Pickwick" the succeeding volume of the "Life and Adventures of Nicholas Nickleby" is the one which would, without reference to its chronological place, call for consideration.

When Mr. Frederick Wedmore asked me to explain some varieties in the Dickens plates which no differences in printing could account for, I replied (see *The Fortnightly Review* for January, 1884), that in some cases Browne made three plates of the same subject, and in etching these he almost unconsciously made little alterations in the design. On further investigation I have, however, ascertained that in the "Nicholas Nickleby" plates fourteen of the subjects were etched no less than four times each, and that these four plates are still in existence. Three of these sets, however, are never used now, and the plates for the "Illustrated Library Edition" are worked from a fine set of the plates which were touched up by "Phiz" soon after Dickens's death and printed in the *édition de luxe* of 1882.

"SUNDAY under Three Heads, by Timothy Sparks," was written by Charles Dickens, and published by Messrs. Chapman and Hall in 1836. It contrasts Sunday as it is, as Sabbath Bills would make it, and as it might be made; and the questions involved are so treated (or perhaps have moved so very little in fifty years) that it might apply equally well to the present day. Besides three illustrations used both on title and cover which are poor and unintelligible, there are three wood engravings occupying the full 12mo. page, but only the second is worthy of preservation on account of its intrinsic value. This represents the incident related of a policeman apprehending a walking-stick vendor on Sunday, and the beginning of a consequent row. There is some indication of power in the composition, and the story is told fairly well. The original drawing of this subject was in a collection in the possession of a Birmingham dealer very recently, and it bore the unconfirmed inscription. "The first drawing for Dickens." "Sunday under Three Heads" has been reprinted in fac-simile by two different publishers, and is sold for a shilling, the original of course being much more valuable. Mr. Fred. Chapman has kindly lent the best engraving for use here.

A Sunday Row.

"NICHOLAS NICKLEBY" was begun in 1837, when Hablôt Browne and Dickens took a journey through the Yorkshire schools to see for themselves the true state of the matters which soon after were exposed to the condemnation of civilisation. The book was completed in one volume, in 1839, after having been published in one shilling monthly parts, like the "Pickwick." For it there were in all sixty-three quarto plates etched for the thirty-nine illustrations, and as each of these carries two designs, there were in all one hundred and twenty-six etched for the publication.

The plate containing the two first subjects, "Ralph Nickleby's first visit to his poor relations," and "Squeers at the Saracen's Head," and the plate with "Newman Noggs leaving the ladies" and "Nicholas astonishes Squeers," were etched twice only. The best illustration, "The Children at their cousin's grave," is drawn in duplicate on one plate and not repeated again. All the other subjects were etched three times at the least, and in the following seven cases each quarto plate, carrying two illustrations, has been done four times. (1) "The Professional Gent at Madame Mantalini's," and " The Country Manager rehearses a combat;" (2) " Affectionate behaviour of Messrs. Pyke and Pluck," and "Nicholas hints at the probability of his leaving the company;" (3) "Linkinwater intimates his approval of Nicholas," and "A sudden recognition, unexpected on both sides;" (4) "Nicholas recognises the young lady unknown," and "The gentleman next door declares his passion for Mrs. Nickleby;" (5) "Nicholas makes his first visit to Mr. Bray," and "The Consultation;" (6) "Mysterious appearance of the gentleman in the small-clothes," and "The last brawl between Sir Mulberry and his pupil;" (7) "Great excitement of Miss Kenwigs at the hair-dresser's shop," and "Nicholas congratulates Arthur Gride on his wedding morning."

In none of these plates are the alterations, or inadvertent changes, so

Mr Ralph Nickleby's first visit to his poor relations

The Yorkshire Schoolmaster at the Saracen's Head

pronounced as in the " Pickwick," and no enumeration of them would help the collector to say that his illustrations are from the first, second, third, or fourth plates. In some cases the steels are distinctly marked; in "The Country Manager rehearses a Combat," there are ordinary numerals, 1, 2, and 3, at the edge of the etching underneath the chair, marking the first three plates, the fourth (the one used in the "Illustrated Library Edition") not being so marked. Many of the illustrations are also marked roughly on the right-hand subject of the two on the quarto plate by strokes **|**, **||**, and **|||**, but as these appear to have been put on after the greater number of impressions was printed they form no guide for ordinary service. As I have already said, the only true test of the quality of the plates is to look carefully through the book, and see if the impressions are well printed. The duplicates vary so little as not to make it seriously worth while to try to get first plates, and in almost all the monthly parts, as well as in the volumes, the impressions from the different plates were promiscuously used by the binder.

The "Nickleby" illustrations vary a good deal in style, those at the beginning being rather better than the later ones. The Squeers plates are all good, as if the designer had had more sympathy with these than with the others. Squeers and the little boy at the Saracen's Head is one of the best-known as well as one of the most successful.

"'Mr. Squeers,' said the waiter, looking in at this juncture, 'here's a gentleman asking for you at the bar.'

"'Show the gentleman in, Richard,' replied Mr. Squeers, in a soft voice.

"'Put your handkerchief in your pocket, you little scoundrel, or I'll murder you when the gentleman goes.'

"The schoolmaster had scarcely uttered these words, in a fierce whisper, when the stranger entered. Affecting not to see him, Mr. Squeers feigned to be intent upon mending a pen, and offering benevolent advice to his youthful pupil."

The repulsive Squeers is perhaps just a very little of a caricature, but not more so than Dickens's inimitable creation. Snawley, the father-in-law of the two new victims of Dotheboys Hall, approaches Squeers with the exact expression of one who was not quite certain of him with whom he was about to deal, and yet with all the low cunning and avarice of the Snawley nature depicted on his unpromising countenance.

The same cannot be said of the other design in the quarto plate, which I introduce merely because it happens to come with the Squeers. It illustrates the following passage :—

> "A lady in deep mourning rose as Mr. Ralph Nickleby entered, but appeared incapable of advancing to meet him, and leant upon the arm of a slight but very beautiful girl of about seventeen, who had been sitting by her. A youth, who appeared a year or two older, stepped forward and saluted Ralph as his uncle.
>
> "'Oh!' growled Ralph, with an ill-favoured frown, 'you are Nicholas, I suppose?'
>
> "'That is my name, sir,' replied the youth.
>
> "'Put my hat down,' said Ralph imperiously. 'Well, ma'am, how do you do? You must bear up against sorrow, ma'am; I always do.'
>
> "'Mine was no common loss,' said Mrs. Nickleby, applying her handkerchief to her eyes.
>
> "'It was no uncommon loss, ma'am,' returned Ralph, as he coolly unbuttoned his spencer. 'Husbands die every day, ma'am, and wives too.'
>
> "'And brothers also, sir,' said Nicholas, with a glance of indignation.
>
> "'Yes, sir, and puppies and pug-dogs, likewise,' replied his uncle, taking a chair."

It can scarcely be said that Kate is made "a very beautiful girl about seventeen," and the drawing of Nicholas is not by any means successful. Ralph Nickleby is the best of the four figures, his cold piercing eye contemptuously resting on his weak-minded sister-in-law.

"The Recognition" is a telling illustration; and the last of all, "The Children at their cousin's grave," is one of the most charming of the series, the old church and trees adding variety to the design. "Great excitement of Miss Kenwigs" and "Nicholas congratulating Arthur Gride," are described in an earlier chapter. Many of the figures in the plates are necessarily vulgar, because of the characters, but there is an unpleasant dwelling on this quality which is not always agreeable. "The Professional Gentleman at Madame Mantalini's" is rendered exceedingly humorous by

the position of the bailiff as seen standing behind the dressmaker's model; the first glance makes it appear as if the officer's waist was about twelve inches in circumference, his big feet appearing underneath in very ludicrous fashion. "Nicholas instructing Smike" is also an excellent plate, the graceful figure of Nicholas contrasting with the crooked lines of the poor pupil.

There are two volumes which, though not usually placed amongst Dickens's works in the series we are now considering, come chronologically into Hablôt Browne's labour at this period. The little 12mo volume, "Sketches of Young Gentlemen," 1838, contains six etched illustrations by "Phiz," which collectors may value as among the artist's sounder work. The figures are not so refined as in many of his later illustrations; and the architectural backgrounds of the first two are really more interesting than the other parts of the design. Two years later the "Sketches of Young Couples," by Dickens, appeared, and in the prints a great advance is made over the "Young Gentlemen." The couple who dote on their children, and the old couple, are executed with more than ordinary care, as the subject suited the artist's pencil. The Kenwigs of "Nicholas Nickleby," which were being illustrated at the same time, are forcibly brought to mind in the couple who dote on their children, and the pictures sketched on the wall in that plate are exceedingly comical.

"Master Humphrey's Clock," embracing the "Old Curiosity Shop" and "Barnaby Rudge," published in 1840-1, was illustrated with wood engravings only. The landscape and architectural designs were mostly drawn by George Cattermole, and the greater number of the figure pieces by Hablôt Browne. The work appeared in three volumes, and it may be said broadly that the illustrations were not by any means satisfactory. In "Ariadne Florentina" Mr. Ruskin abuses them roundly, and Mr. George Augustus Sala has done the same. It must be admitted there is reason for their dissatisfaction, for the unmitigated vulgarity of many of the figures is very objectionable. Some of the cuts are, however, worthy of admiration, and those used to embellish this book are the best of the series.

"Old Weller and his Grandson" (used at page 80) is an excellent continuation on wood of "Phiz's" portrait of Sam's father in "Pickwick." "Barnaby and the Raven" (page 106) is one of the few Mr. Ruskin can bring himself to admire. The "Barnaby Rudge" tailpiece (used at page 148) is very cleverly drawn, and "Barnaby and his Mother" is one of the finest creations of a character amongst the illustrations. The frontispieces to the volumes (used at pages 115 and 119) are also engravings involving great labour, even after the first completed thoughts of the designer were carried out. The "Death of Quilp" and "The Rioters" are admirable illustrations to the story, the loneliness and horribleness of Quilp's death being intensified by the melancholy waters and the tortured attitude of the dead dwarf. Two blocks prepared for the original edition, but never used, are printed here and for the first time.

A little later "Phiz" made drawings to illustrate "Master Humphrey's Clock," which were published separately as plates with Dickens's permission. Four were for the "Old Curiosity Shop" and four for "Barnaby Rudge;" but they are not so successful as many of his later works, and not so good as those done separately in a similar way (see page 127) to illustrate "Dombey and Son."

The variations of the plates for "Martin Chuzzlewit" (1842) are not difficult to explain. All the subjects were etched on quarto plates, two as usual on each, and it is remarkable that without exception all the subjects are placed upright. This was the same in the "Pickwick" and "Nickleby" plates, as it was not until the "Coming home from Church" in "Dombey" that an oblong subject was introduced into Dickens's works. Five of the quarto plates in "Chuzzlewit" were etched three times, and the

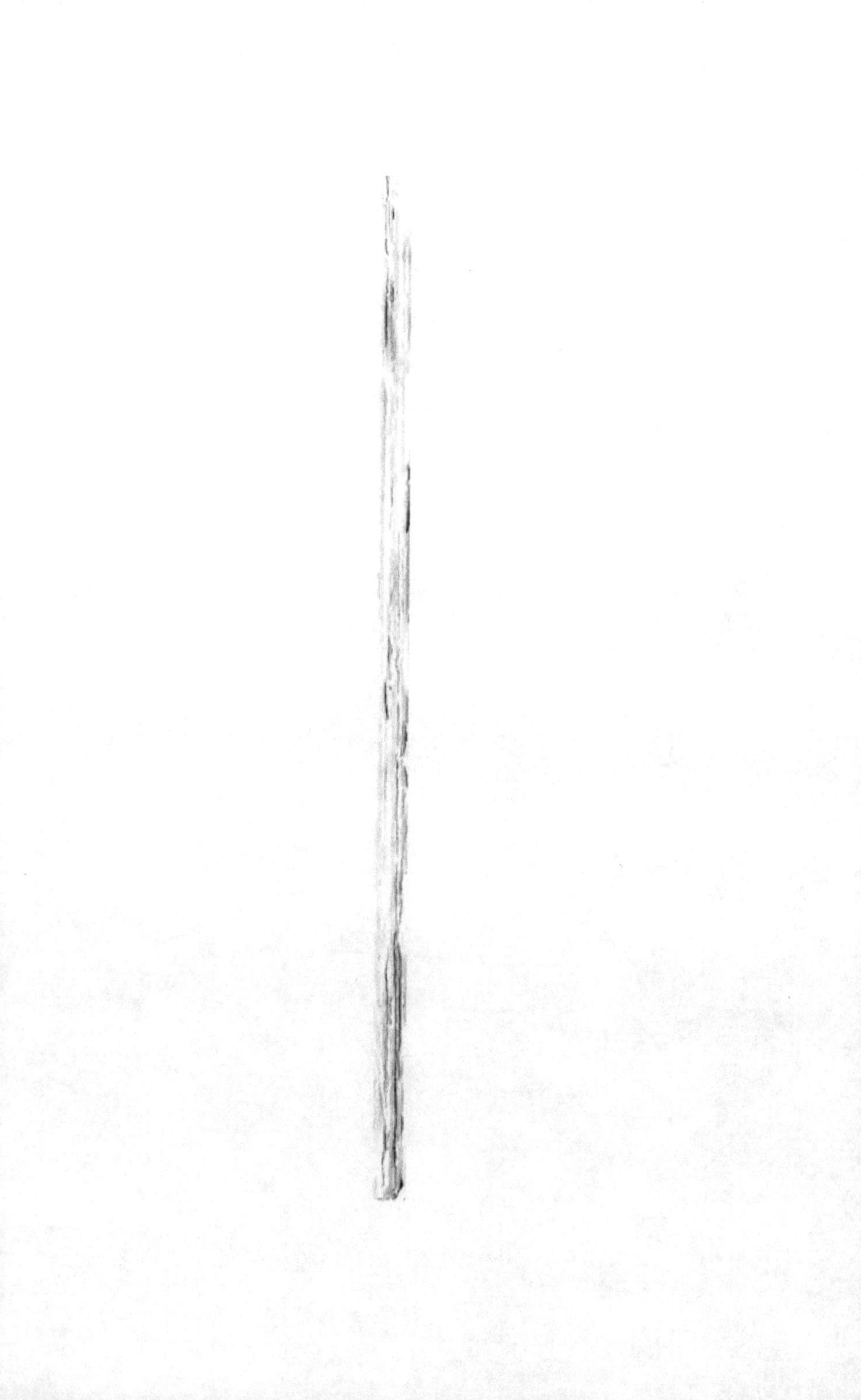

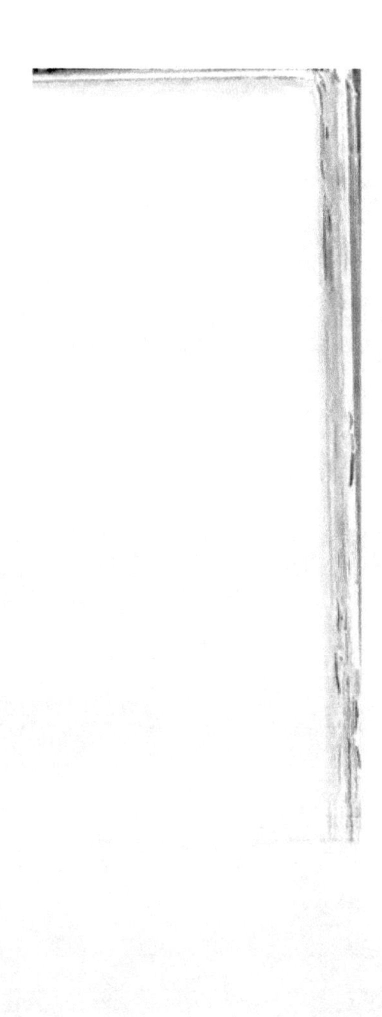

remainder in duplicate only. The five are (1) the frontispiece and title-page, (2) " Meekness of Pecksniff," and " Martin Chuzzlewit suspects the Land-lady; " (3) " Mr. Pinch and the new pupil," and " Mark begins to be jolly; " (4) " Mr. Nadgett breathes an atmosphere of mystery," and " Mr. Pinch departs to seek his fortune; " and (5) " Pleasant little family party at Mr. Pecksniff's " and " Pinch starts homeward with the new pupil." There are also some minute differences in the subjects as they appear in the plates, but none of any real importance. In " Easy Shaving " the bill beside the pole has writing, and in the other a female figure ; in the plate with the written bill the figure is placed on the other side of the etching. In the " Meekness of Pecksniff " two of the boxes on the mantelshelf are inscribed " Poor Box," while in one of the plates (that used in the " Illustrated Library Edition ") it is unmarked. In two of the plates of " Mark begins to be jolly " the signboard about the blacksmith is blank, and in the third it is filled in " A Blacksmith."

The " Martin Chuzzlewit " illustrations, though not so refined as the " Dombey " and " Copperfield," are a marked improvement on the slightly vulgar " Nicholas Nickleby " etchings. Pecksniff is in every case quite the realisation of the novelist's character, and he is kept up excellently through-out the book. " Truth prevails and virtue is triumphant " is one of the cleverest. This plate also carries another representation of Pecksniff, " Mr. Todgers and the Pecksniffs call upon Miss Pinch." " Mr. Pecksniff discharges a Duty he owes to Society " and " Mr. Muddle is both particular and peculiar in his attentions," are very good designs ; and the " Mercy " of " Balm for the wounded Orphan " is prettier and more like the character in the story than any of her other portraits. " Mrs. Gamp propoges a Toast," the celebrated plate, is used in our first chapter. " Mr. Pinch departs to seek his fortune " is singularly fortunate in the action of the horse of the smaller vehicle. " Martin meets an acquaintance at the house of a mutual relation " (here reproduced) is one of the most sketchy " Phiz " did for the series.

IKE the others, the "Dombey" plates, began in 1846, were published in the monthly parts and completed in 1848. They are forty in number, and without exception were etched in duplicate. The greater number were drawn on quarto plates, having two subjects on each as usual, but the frontispiece, the last four illustrations, and the duplicates of three others were etched singly on steels of octavo size.* These duplicates do not vary in any perceptible degree. The one where the most variation is visible is "Abstraction and Recognition." In this the bills pasted on the wall beside Alice in one plate are less mutilated than in the other, a difference almost too trifling to mention.

In the second chapter I have said a good deal in connection with some of the illustrations to "Dombey" when they were first drawn, and two of the best plates are there introduced. Another plate is interesting as much because of difference in style as for its fine artistic treatment, as mentioned in the chapter dealing with the methods of etching employed by Hablôt Browne. The illustration, "On the Dark Road," is a plate on which a tint had first been placed by means of a ruling-machine; and by a process of "stopping out" and "burnishing out" an effect equivalent to mezzotint was obtained. Notwithstanding the number of impressions taken from it, the plate is still in fair condition, and having been very carefully printed by Mr. Yates for this work, little or none of the original beauty is gone. The original drawing, it should be mentioned, is very rough and crude, having only a mere indication of the design; the horses, however, are well drawn and clearer than the rest of the drawing. The subject is Carker on his flight from Dijon, after the meeting with Edith, when he thinks every sound tells of an avenger following close on his heels. "Shame, disappointment, and discomfiture gnawed at his heart; a constant apprehension of being overtaken oppressed him heavily."

"Phiz" had a good deal of trouble in realising "Dombey" to Dickens's

---

* An American edition published in 1844 has fourteen cleverly etched copies of the plates.

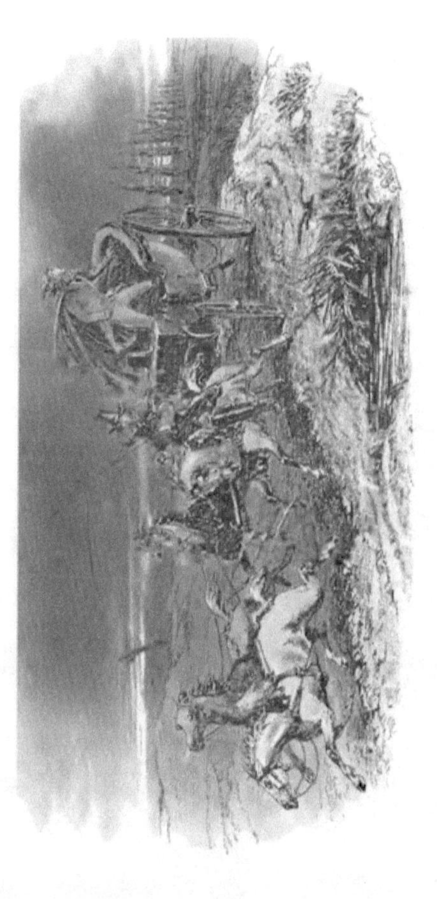

satisfaction, and submitted a number of sketches before a decision as to his style could be settled. The likeness is not kept up entirely throughout the series. Dombey is hit off very well in "The Christening Party," and this etching and the one alongside it in the same quarto plate, "Polly rescues the Charitable Grinder," present a remarkable contrast in subject, composition, drawing, and character. The urchin leaping the post is the very antithesis to the stately Mr. Dombey, and it is an example of the versatility of Hablôt Browne's genius that on one and the same plate he could give such different characteristics while preserving his individuality.

Hitherto all the illustrations for Dickens's works were upright in shape, but in "Dombey" the rule was broken through, and "Coming from Church" was the first published in an oblong form. Upright illustrations are of course preferred by the reader, as saving him the trouble of turning the book, but so many subjects can be better treated as oblongs that it is almost a wonder that neither in "Pickwick," "Nicholas Nickleby," nor "Martin Chuzzlewit" the necessity which arose in "Dombey" was made manifest.*

The illustrations to "Dombey" show a still further improvement in the art of "Phiz," and nearly equal the "Copperfield" and "Bleak House" plates of a few years later. One difficulty Browne had to contend with was that Dickens was living at Lausanne, in Switzerland, and the sketches had to be sent out to him. It caused great delay as well as trouble in understanding any suggestions the author had to make in returning the drawings to the artist.

At the time of the publication of "Dombey" as a complete volume (1848) "Phiz" published eight full-length etched portraits for further illustrating the volume, which were sold separately in green covers at two shillings each set. They were issued under the sanction of Dickens, and represented Dombey and Carker, Miss Tox, Mrs. Skewton, Mrs. Pipchin, Old Sol

* It is not out of place here to remind publishers that all the oblong plates in Dickens's works are on right-hand pages, with titles facing outwards, and that the custom of making all oblong illustrations, however placed, to read inwards, causing the reader annoyance in turning the book, is indefensible.

and Captain Cuttle, "Old Joe, Sir," Miss Nipper and Polly. The best of them is Polly, standing amidst her children in an unaffected, simple attitude, extremely winning. Four were also very beautifully engraved on steel by Mr. Robert Young and published separately. These plates have recently been reprinted, and connoisseurs should be careful in purchasing to see that they obtain the original sets printed under the artist's own directions.

A Top Sawyer.

The illustrations to "David Copperfield" are so splendidly sustained throughout that it is almost impossible, without naming the greater number of the plates, to refer to those which really deserve distinction. The hero, David Copperfield, is, as he should be, the character with which the illustrator has taken most care: as a boy he is ever a little gentleman and a loveable being, his portrait being quite equal to Dickens's charming description. In the plate "I make myself known to my Aunt," given in Chapter I., we have probably the best illustration in the book, and one of the finest "Phiz" ever etched. Running it very closely are the two, "The friendly waiter and I" and "My magnificent order at the public-house," in both of which David is as perfect a realisation of the text as can be imagined.

These drawings are, indeed, something more than this: they are graphic creations of character quite as much as Dickens's written descriptions are. The waiter is such a man as may still be seen in old-fashioned places, and though his dress has changed in go-ahead cities, his easy imposition on the simple and unwary is still thoroughly characteristic of his race. The good landlord and his kind lady in the other plate (even though not placed quite in the position mentioned in the letterpress) are full of that

human kindness which makes the heart warm to them, though they have nothing to do with the story; and this, of course, is through the illustrator's invention and genius alone, quite independent of the author.

"The friendly waiter and I" illustrates the following portion of the story :—

"'There's half a pint of ale for you. Will you have it now?'

"I thanked him, and said 'Yes.' Upon which he poured it out of a jug into a large tumbler, and held it up against the light, and made it look beautiful.

"'My eye!' he said. 'It seems a good deal, don't it?'

"'It does seem a good deal,' I answered with a smile. For it was delightful to me to find him so pleasant. He was a twinkling-eyed, pimple-faced man, with his hair standing upright all over his head; and as he stood with one arm a-kimbo, holding up the glass to the light with other hand, he looked quite friendly."

Being on a quarto plate, this is accompanied by "My musical breakfast," representing the scene as follows :—

"I sat down to my brown loaf, my eggs, and my rasher of bacon, with a basin of milk besides, and made a most delicious meal. While I was yet in full enjoyment of it, the old woman of the house said to the master—

"'Have you got your flute with you?'

"'Yes,' he returned.

"'Have a blow at it,' said the old woman, coaxingly. 'Do!'

"The master upon this put his hand underneath the skirts of his coat and brought out his flute in three pieces, which he screwed together, and began immediately to play."

"My magnificent order at the public-house" realises the passage—

"'What is your best—your VERY BEST—ale a glass?' For it was a special occasion. I don't know what. It may have been my birthday.

"'Twopence-halfpenny,' says the landlord, 'is the price of the Genuine Stunning ale.'

"'Then,' says I, producing the money, 'just draw me a glass of the Genuine Stunning, if you please, with a good head to it.'

"The landlord looked at me in return over the bar, from head to foot, with a strange smile on his face; and instead of drawing the beer, looked round the screen and said something to his wife. She came out from behind it, with her work in her hand, and joined him in surveying me. Here we stand, all three, before me now.

The landlord in his shirt-sleeves, leaning against the bar window-frame; his wife, looking over the little half-door; and I, in some confusion, looking up at them from outside the partition."

This plate carries two subjects, the second representing David's departure from Yarmouth.

"When we were all in a bustle outside the door, I found that Mr. Peggotty was prepared with an old shoe, which was to be thrown after us for luck, and which he offered to Mrs. Gummidge for that purpose.

"'No, it had better be done by somebody else, Dan'l,' said Mrs. Gummidge. 'I'm a lone lorn creatur myself, and everything that reminds me of creaturs that ain't lone and lorn goes contrairy with me.'

"'Come, old gal!' cried Mr. Peggotty, 'take and heave it!'

"'No, Dan'l,' returned Mrs. Gummidge, whimpering and shaking her head. 'If I felt less, I could do more. You don't feel like me, Dan'l; things don't go contrairy with you, nor you with them; you had better do it yourself.'

"But here Peggotty, who had been going about from one to another in a hurried way, kissing everybody, called out from the cart in which we all were by this time Em'ly and I on two little chairs side by side), that Mrs. Gummidge must do it. So Mrs. Gummidge did it, and, I am sorry to relate, cast a damp upon the festive character of our departure by immediately bursting into tears."

"Steerforth and Mr. Mell," "I am Married," and "Our Pew at Church," are filled to repletion with delineations of varied characters, and are practically inexhaustible under examination. Purely artistic effects are not wanting in the Rembrandtesque "Wanderer," and the most charming vignette on the title-page. Caricature further lends its aid to enhance the interest of the illustrations, and Micawber and Traddles's attitudes when "We are disturbed in our cookery," and "Mr. Micawber delivers some valedictory remarks," are sources of never-ending merriment. Another plate worthy of special mention is "Uriah Heep and Littimer in prison," where the philanthropists (!) confer with the two hypocrites.

The plates for "David Copperfield" were etched in two full sets. But, unlike many of the others, those of the set used in the *édition de luxe* and the "Illustrated Library Edition," are not in nearly so good condition as those

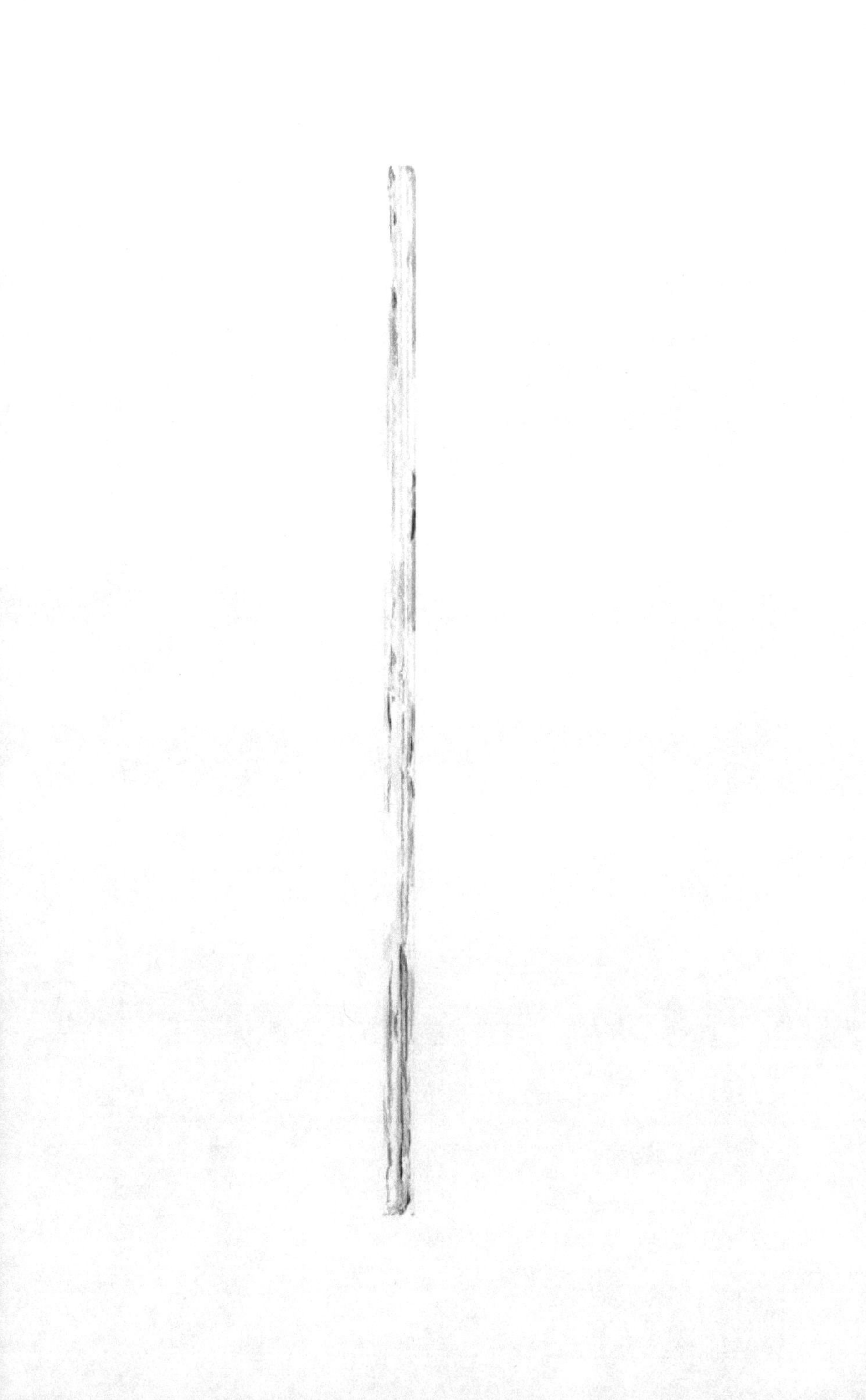

OLD
ALE

which have not been used since the original publication. About half of the etchings were executed on octavo steels having one subject only, the other half being on quarto plates, as usual carrying two subjects. In several cases illustrations on quarto plates in one of the sets are in the other singly on octavo plates. They vary very little in detail, the duplicates being almost identical.

The only decided failure in the "Copperfield" series is the figure of Agnes, which is never nearly up to the beautiful character described by Dickens. "Phiz" is more successful with the womenfolk, and "Martha" and Peggotty, and Dora's maiden aunts, are always good; it is only when "Phiz" has to draw a lady in an ordinary ladylike attitude that he comparatively fails.

HAT "Mervyn Clitheroe" is to Ainsworth's and Lever's books, "Bleak House" is to the Dickens series. There is more variety in it than in any of the others, and the quality throughout is very high. Landscapes and architectural pieces enter largely into the illustrations, and the boisterousness of the earlier comic plates by "Phiz" is toned down, though not perhaps altogether to advantage.

The method of ruling the plate and producing a mezzotint effect, first tried in the "Dark Road" of "Dombey and Son" and again in "The River" scene of "David Copperfield," is now employed in no less than nine subjects, and with undoubted success in every instance. The most striking of these is the plate called "The Morning," with Esther's poor mother lying at the graveyard gateway. Weirdness, horror, and loneliness are the characteristics of the design, which is one of the best Hablôt Browne ever did. It goes a long step farther than the description in the letterpress, excellent though it be, and has done much more to realise the painful sentiment of the story.

Another design which perhaps is still further now a part of the story in every one's mind, is "Consecrated Ground," where Jo points out the "hallowed" resting-place of Esther's father, who was always, Jo said, "so wery good to me, he wos."

This plate being in quarto carries with it "The Dancing School," where Caddy's betrothed is busily engaged giving lessons to the flowerets of thirty years ago, and "Deportment" standing before the fire patronising the proceedings.

The Guppy plates are all very good and relieve the book with their humour. "*In Re* Guppy. Extraordinary Proceedings," and "Guppy's Desolation" are ludicrous enough, yet without exaggeration, and explain the story without difficulty. The mezzotints, which all come at the end, are magnificent productions, and I should have liked to have given them all here. "A new Meaning in the Roman" and "The Shadow," with their dreadful associations, are very impressive, while the grace and beauty of the "Nurse and Patient" is a striking contrast to the subject in the same quarto plate, "The Appointed Time," where Guppy and Tony discover the result of spontaneous combustion. The "Nurse and Patient" is as delightful a feminine subject as "Phiz" ever drew; there is something more refined in it than usual in his drawings of ladies, and it is about the highest Art he ever reached in that class of subject.

The only duplicate plates for "Bleak House" are the nine machined and mezzotinted octavo plates towards the end of the book and the frontispiece. All the others were etched once only, about half of them being on octavo plates and the remainder on quarto.

A Signature of "Phiz."

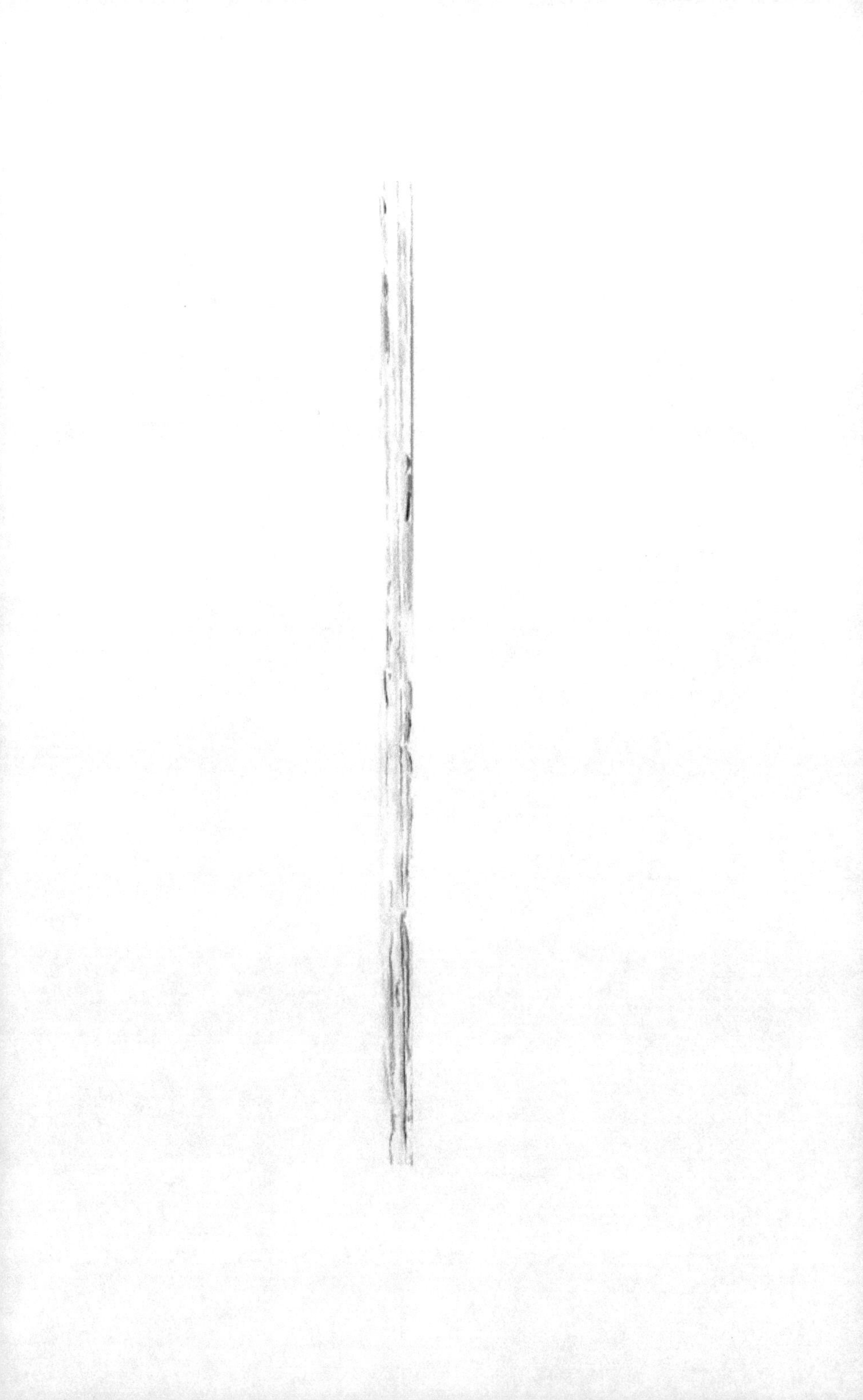

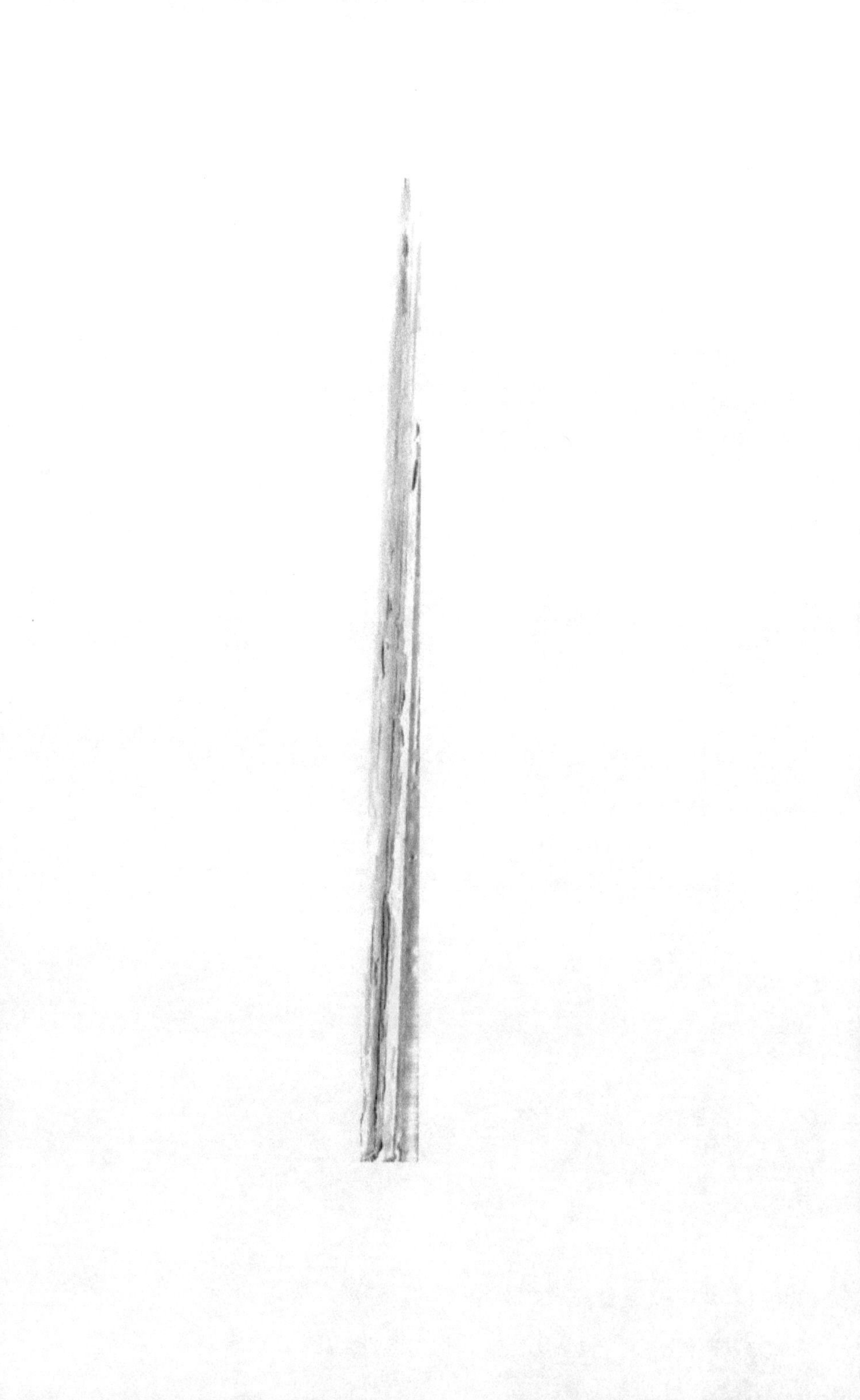

EFORE a couple of years had passed after the completion of "Bleak House" the monthly parts of "Little Dorrit" began to make their appearance, and between 1855 and 1857 it was issued in the way Dickens had again made so popular. In the series there is a lack of supported effort on the part of the illustrator which makes itself apparent several times. For instance, the "Reception of an Old Friend" does not at all carry out the amazement and horror spoken of in the story when Mr. Dorrit assaults young John, and the figures are ill-drawn. Others again are charming specimens of the etching work of "Phiz," and the two here printed for contrast on one page (though originally on different steels), "The Ferry" and "Floating Away," are very beautiful examples of his Art in landscape representation. These subjects were etched on ruled plates, on which the burnisher was freely used. One is light and airy with sunshine and trees and pleasant water; the other is dark and heavy, with moonlight only partly illumining the deep-toned landscape and Clennam launching his roses on the flowing river bound for the "eternal seas." "The Marshalsea becomes an Orphan" is another fine illustration, and is done on quarto, with "Society expressing itself on a question of Marriage," the latter representing Mrs. Merdle and Mrs. Gowan discussing how men should look on matrimony and what society thinks of the union they are then discussing. "The Marshalsea becomes an Orphan," with one of its figures so like Mr. John Bright, is thus described in the volume:—

"Twelve o'clock having just struck, and the carriage being reported ready in the outer courtyard, the brothers Dorrit proceeded downstairs arm-in-arm. Edward Dorrit, Esquire (once Tip), and his sister Fanny followed, also arm-in-arm; Mr. Plornish and Maggy, to whom had been entrusted the removal of such of the family effects as were considered worth removing, followed, bearing bundles and burdens to be packed in a cart."

Dickens was living at Boulogne during part of the time the plates for "Little Dorrit" were in hand, and on July 2, 1856, he wrote to Browne that he was returning thither the next day, and asking him to make the " Pensioner Entertainment " illustration "as characteristic as ever you please, my little dear, but quiet." Again on February 10, 1857, Dickens wrote as follows from Tavistock House, the letter now belonging to Mr. Robert Young :—

" MY DEAR BROWNE,—In the dinner scene it is highly important that Mr. Dorrit should not be too comic. He is too comic now. He is described in the text as ' shedding tears,' and what he imperatively wants is an expression doing less violence in the reader's mind to what is going to happen to him, and much more in accordance with that serious end which is so close before him.

" Pray do not neglect this change.   " Yours faithfully, C. D."

This instruction was duly attended to and Mr. Dorrit made not by any means comic, but quite pathetic, the design being one of the fullest and best in the book.

On the 6th of March, 1857, Dickens again writes to " Phiz " that the drawings submitted of " Flora's Tour of Inspection " and " Mr. Merdle a Borrower," were " very good subjects—both," and adding, " I can't distinctly make out the detail, but I take Sparkles to be getting the tortoiseshell knife from the box ; am I right ? " The same letter contains a pencil note by Hablôt Browne that as he could not get up to London he would send the plate to Mr. Young by rail.

Of the forty illustrations, thirty-six are on octavo plates, having one subject on each, and there are three quarto plates with two on each—the frontispiece and title, " The Travellers " and " The Dignity is affronted," and the plate printed here. Eight of the plates are machine engraved, and are full of fine colour, five of these being in duplicate probably because these mezzotinted plates wear more quickly than ordinary etchings. In duplicate are " The Birds in the Cage," " The Room with the Portrait," " The Ferry," " Visitors at the Works," and " Floating Away." The differences in these are small and are of no importance as guides to the collector, nor do they affect the quality of the illustrations.

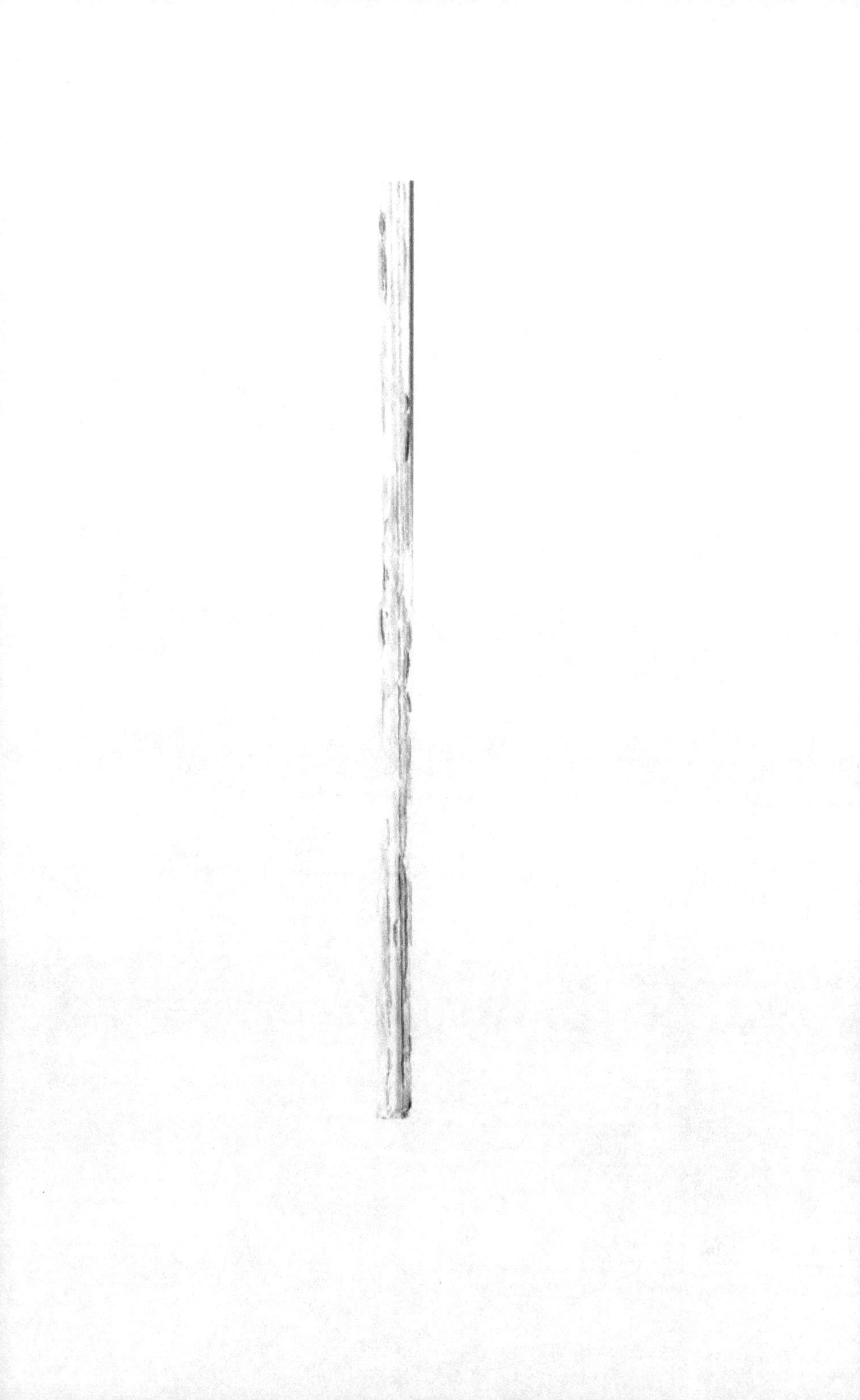

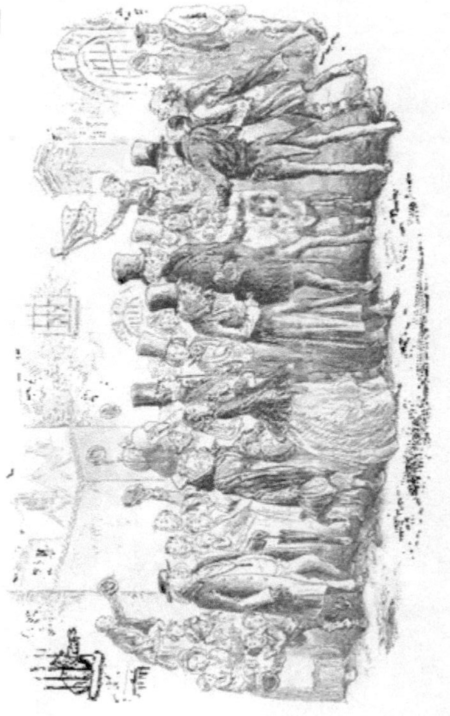

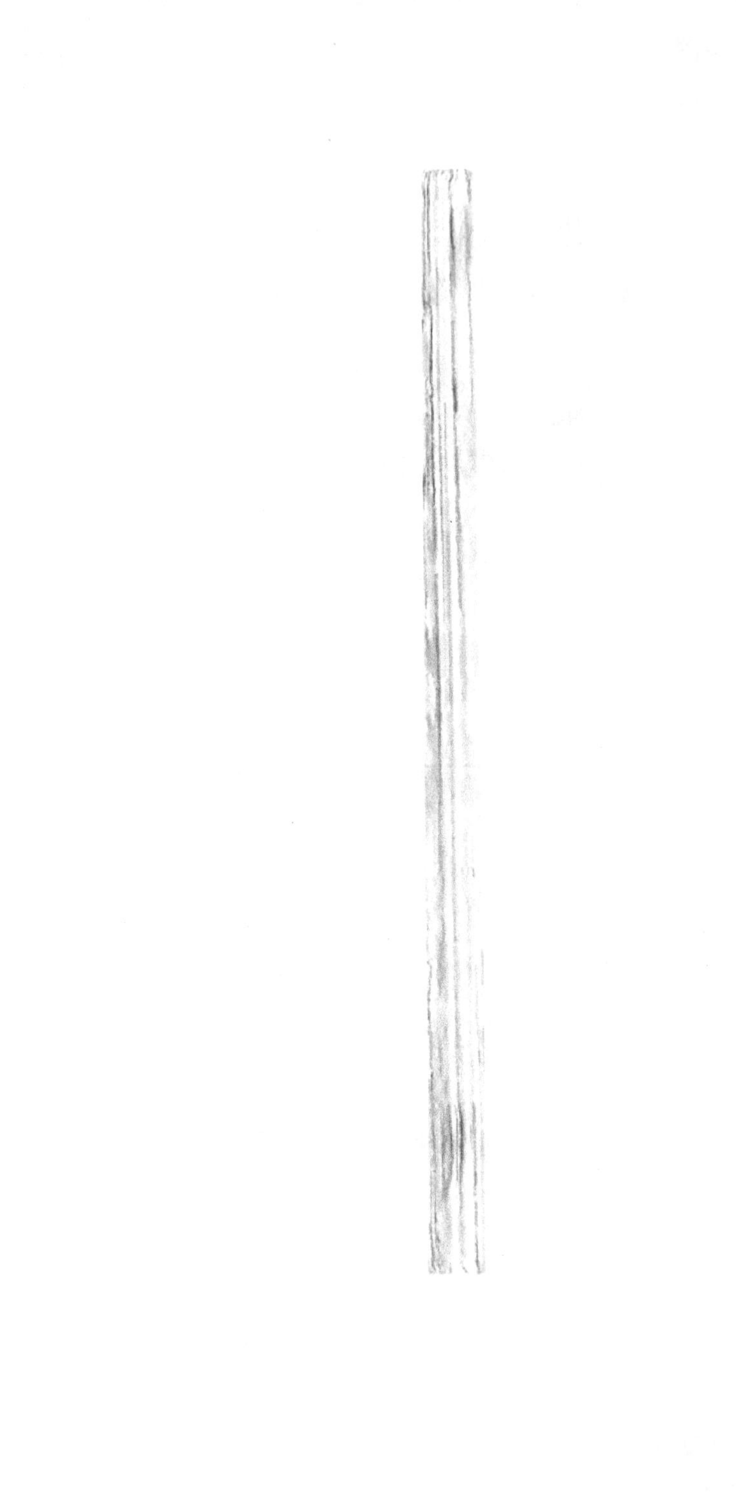

The last book which "Phiz" illustrated for Dickens was the "Tale of Two Cities," published in 1859. These were only single plates—eight in all, carrying sixteen illustrations—none being prepared in duplicate. The illustrations are fairly well drawn, and with an evidently facile pencil. The English people represented are characteristic of the period, but the same cannot be said of the French pictures. The latter are English clad in partly French style, but there is little attempt at archæological correctness in the costumes. In "The Sea Rises," otherwise a capital etching, we have English figures gesticulating like French ones, but no one without the letterpress could affirm that their nationality was French. The drawing on this plate is a little exaggerated, the touch of caricature taking away from the extreme gravity which ought to pervade such an occurrence.

The most successful of the sixteen illustrations is "The Likeness," where the remarkable resemblance between the characters is heightened by the aid of good pictorial Art. "The Woman in the Wine-shop" is one of "Phiz's" pretty women, and the fear in the faces of the accomplices is cleverly etched. "The Knock at the Door" is another dramatic incident very ably rendered. All the illustrations, with the exception of the frontispiece and title, are oblong.

"Phiz" did no more work for Dickens after the plates for the "Tale of Two Cities." It does not appear that there was any actual rupture between the novelist and the artist who had so long and so honourably been associated with him. The choice of an illustrator for the next book, "Our Mutual Friend," seems to have been decided by circumstances unconnected with Hablôt Browne. In Dickens's letters there is one addressed to Messrs. Longmans, the publishers, in which he introduces "young Marcus Stone" to them, and hopes they will be able to give him some illustrating work to do, both because of the recent death of Mr. Stone's father and of his own cleverness. And it is probable that partly from a desire to help the artist and partly from a legitimate desire for change, Dickens employed another illustrator for " Our Mutual Friend." From this time the decline of " Phiz" was very marked in public estimation, and if Dickens had thoroughly realised how much his change would embitter the latter years of one who had so ably helped him in previous times, it is certainly doubtful if the change would have been made.

Old Humphrey sleeping.

" Wedding Breakfasts provided." From an advertisement in " *The Times*, such as they are," 1862.

CHAPTER V.

THE ILLUSTRATIONS FOR THE WORKS OF LEVER.

CONTEMPORARY with the publication of Dickens's novels, two other writers were engaged in similar labours and, like Dickens, from time to time published romances in monthly parts at one shilling each. Lever was almost an exact contemporary of Charles Dickens, but Ainsworth (the illustrations to whose works are considered in the succeeding chapter) began later.

Charles Lever made his reputation with " The Con-fessions of Harry Lorrequer " and " Charles O'Malley," rollicking Irish stories full of humour and interspersed with song. The character of story-teller of Hibernian people remained with him long after he had entered and conquered new fields of romance, and, in fact, remains connected with his name to this day.

Wrapper novels, after Messrs. Chapman and Hall had discovered their new hold on the public, grew rapidly into favour with publishers. Dickens's books were always clad in green, as symbolical, it has been suggested, of his inexhaustible freshness.　Thackeray presented his novels in yellow, typical of the biliousness and slightly unhealthy feeling in his magnificently written but unsatisfying publications; while Lever's monthly parts appeared in a pink covering, indicative, it has also been said, of his never-failing warmth and buoyancy.　Lever, Dr. Fitzpatrick tells us, " was fastidious in regard to the designs of 'Phiz' on his monthly wrappers," and said that there was a great deal in the externals of a book as well as of a gentleman.

It is from Dr. Fitzpatrick's excellent " Life of Charles Lever " that most is to be learned regarding the various transactions between the author and the illustrator.　There are not, however, many direct references to " Phiz " even there, though now and again the illustrations are alluded to, and that not always in a complimentary manner.　At one place the writer speaks of the etching printed here, " Lorrequer practising physic," as richly illustrating a most comical incident in the " Confessions," while at another he alludes to the criticism of Lever's brother that the illustrations for " Jack Hinton " are a little muddy and confused, and that " Phiz " always succeeded best with single figures or a group of three—a very erroneous estimate, as a glance through this book will show.

In a note at the same place in Dr. Fitzpatrick's book, a letter from Browne is quoted which gives the account elsewhere alluded to of his destruction of much valuable correspondence.

" Living as he (Lever) did abroad, our correspondence was generally confined to the etchings we had on at the time.　Some years ago, when I was about to remove from Croydon, I had a bonfire to lessen the lumber, and burnt a stock of papers containing all Lever's, Dickens's, Ainsworth's, and other authors' notes.　As they were almost solely about illustrations, I did not at the time attach any importance to them, nor did I think that any one else would ; but I was afterwards blamed by several autograph collectors for my wilful destruction of what they considered valuable."

Rough drawings, being mostly mere indications of the subject, were made for the Lever illustrations, but no complete sets of them exist in the

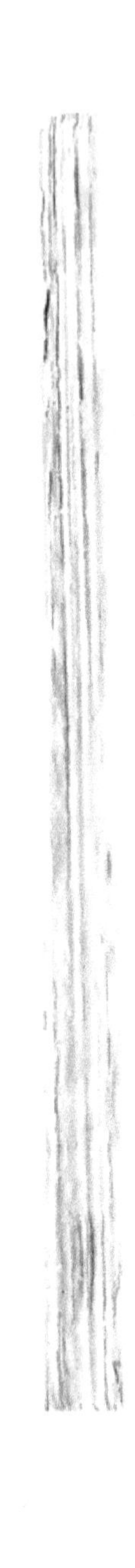

same way as of the Dickens drawings. A number of them were sold at The Fine Art Society's exhibition in 1883 and went to different collectors, but there is nothing in the sketches to call for special or detailed examination. A number of these drawings, it may be remarked, however, still remain in the possession of the artist's family.

Charles Lever's first book, " The Confessions of Harry Lorrequer," was issued in 1839 with twenty-two plates by " Phiz." Although Browne was considered by Lever (and Lever's brother, who took a good deal upon himself in the way of criticism) to have done some of the later volumes much better, it may be said on review of the whole series that not one of the volumes is better illustrated than " Harry Lorrequer." The objection may be raised, and with some justice, that " Phiz" gave the work an appearance of unnecessary noise and bustle, as he delighted in making his pictures representations of the more uproarious scenes, but, on the other hand, it cannot be doubted that the rollicking pictures had much to do with the first success of the novel as a publication.

The most remarkable picture in the book is " The Supper at Father Malachi's;" a real incident it is said, and one at which the prototype of the priest did not know whether to laugh or scold. Here all is riot and uproar: everyone is more or less excited with liquor; the song of " The Battle of the Boyne" has called out the pugilistic tendencies of the Irishmen assembled, and the fun (as shown in the plate printed here) grows fast and furious. " Mr. Cudmore filling the teapot," is admirable as illustrating the text, though a little "stupid" artistically. In connection with the latter the name of "Phiz" is mentioned in the novel: Tom O'Flaherty makes the too self-conscious Cudmore believe he has performed a menial action in pouring out tea (the incident illustrated), and urges him to resent the indignity. " The expression of increasing wonder and surprise depicted on Mr. Cudmore's face at these words my friend 'Phiz' might convey; I cannot venture to describe it." But "Phiz" did not see it, and the point goes unillustrated. "Lorrequer practising physic" is (as shown in our plate) a grand realisation of the text, and the writhing of the patient under the quack's touch, the worshipping air of the local doctors, and the gravity and apparently profound wisdom of the pretended physician, are in the artist's happiest style. This, with "Mr. Burke's enthusiasm for the Duke of Wellington," is also printed here. "Dr. Finucane and the Grey Mare" was a true incident, as related in Lever's life. "Mr. Burke's enthusiasm for the Duke of Wellington" is another capital illustration.

The next book of Lever's published in the same way as "Lorrequer" was "Charles O'Malley," completed in 1841. It contains forty-four etchings in the two volumes, and is a contrast to "Humphrey's Clock," finished about the same time. Nearly every illustration is successful. "A Flying Shot," "Charley trying a Charger," and "The Two Chesnuts," contain horses, and are all admirably drawn, the horses in moving attitudes most difficult of representing. The last shows O'Malley and Baby Blake with their spanking pair of chesnuts outrunning the mail. The original drawing for this now belongs to Mr. Frank Barnard, a worthy wearer of the illustrator's mantle. A cut of the same subject is used in Dicks' English Novels, and an impression from it is inserted at page 45 of this work.

The plate of "Baby Blake," turning round from the piano and smiling, is one of the pretty women "Phiz" could easily draw in his best days, and one of the nicest of these, for the figure is really as charming as described. It is printed here. Many of the other plates will well repay a little study, and although they are perhaps even more uproarious in their humour than the story itself, the exaggeration is pardonable. The drunken frolics, ever a favourite subject with "Phiz," are expounded with more than ordinary attention and pleasure.

"Our Mess," in three volumes, followed, consisting of "Jack Hinton the Guardsman" in one volume, and "Tom Burke" in two, all dated 1844, when completed. "Jack Hinton" has twenty-six etched plates and nineteen wood-

Lorrequer practising Physic

Mr Burke's enthusiasm for the Duke of Wellington.

"Ruby Blake"

cuts, amongst them being some of the best representations of running horses "Phiz" has done; "Father Tom's Curriculum," "La Vivandière," the "Four-in-Hand," and "Modirideroo," being in the numbers. "Irish Sport with a Cockney" is humorous, and "Farewell to Tipperary Joe" is a statuesque figure, with regret depicted on every line of his doleful attitude. The woodcuts are mostly small and are all remarkably clever, and a decided advance on "Humphrey's Clock" of 1841. "Tim on a Donkey" is very humorous; "The Boys of the Hotel Rooney" is somewhat in the key that Mr. Herkomer painted his "Casual Ward," and "Tipperary Joe carried on a door" is a good specimen of the best "Phiz" wood engravings.

"Tom Burke of Ours" is not quite so successful, the biting-in of the plates being unequal and in many cases far too heavy. The best plates are "The Struggle," "The wondrous effect of a Piper's pipe of tobacco," with a multitude of small figures, "Minette receiving the Legion of Honour," and "The Death of Minette." "The Drummer who did not mind a hole in the skin," "Fighting their battles over again," and "Mdlle. de Lacostellère" are also good, the latter a graceful representation of an elegant, dark-haired dancer. Napoleon, who is drawn several times, is recognisable in the plates, but is scarcely sufficiently emperor-like; but "Darby in the Chair," printed here, is one of the best. This shows the witness sitting upon the chair in the centre of the court, as is the Irish custom, looking round with an expression such as Sam Weller may be imagined to have had when counsel tried vainly to bamboozle him. "The Attorney's Office," accompanying it, is also clever.

The twenty-six plates to "The O'Donoghue" (1845) did not add to the fame of "Phiz." There is an element of caricature of the Irish not quite pleasant even to their enemies, and which does not appear in other books to the same extent. It is said that Lever found it difficult sometimes to keep Browne from caricaturing his Irish characters, and in "The O'Donoghue" the charge is well founded. It is even said that Lever attributed some aspersions he had had cast on him (that his Irish people were always exaggerated) to some of the plates by " Phiz." They are clever enough, but somewhat theatrical in their grouping, and do not always strictly accord with the text. At the same time all the plates do not fall under the same condemnation, and the etching " Frederick and Mark" has a beautifully drawn horse and is a fine composition throughout.

Dr. Fitzpatrick tells the amusing story of a mistake which occurred with the title of one of " The O'Donoghue" illustrations. " Phiz " wrote to Lever to explain how the lengthy and ridiculous title came to appear, saying :—

> " As to myself, when I saw it I was convulsed with laughter. I do not know whether to attribute the mistake to the carelessness, stupidity, inebriety, or the practical joking peculiarities of the writing engraver. I think it is a compound. Orr [the publisher] sent to me for a title to the plate, and as I was rather at a loss to name the child I wrote on a slip of paper thus :—1 'Mark recognises an old acquaintance,' or simply 2 'The Glen,' or, (addressing Orr) anything else you like, my little dears—meaning that Orr might give a better if he could, and behold the writing engraver makes a Chinese copy of the whole."

The title on the etching, therefore, appeared as follows, gravely written in two lines across the plate: " Mark recognises an old acquaintance, or The Glen, or anything else you like, my little dears." It is the last in " The O'Donoghue," published in 1845.

" The Knight of Gwynne" (1847), a tale of Ireland at the time of the Union, has forty illustrations, mostly of amusing Irish incidents, which give full scope for the artist's power of drawing humorous figures. It is notable, as in many other of the books " Phiz " illustrated, that the subjects chosen for the plates are nearly all capable of representing the coarser side of the characters of the story, or with elaborated designs full of figures, or Irishmen in conclave or in trouble. The best of the etchings are " The Ibis Hunt," where the mock dromedary becomes thirsty and strikes for a drink; "Sandy McGrane

Darby in the Chair

expedites the doctor" (both printed here) ; "Daly and his Friends," the queer Irish Indian chieftain, followed in the streets by an admiring crowd of Irishmen ; "Daly bestows a helmet on Bully Dodd," the half-treacherous, half-humorous type of Irishman being given at full length; "Dodd and Dempsey at the Review," and "Mr. Paul tastes Mrs. Fumbally's ' you know, you know,' " with its wonderful funny portraits on the wall.

"The Confessions of Con Cregan," understood to be by Lever, though not so stated in the book itself, appeared in two volumes in 1849. It is carefully illustrated in both steel and wood. In the twenty-nine plates the illustrator has ample scope to display his powers of invention, as the subjects go over a wide range: horses, students' riots, society pictures, domestic, comic, and serious, and Spanish subjects, with pirate incidents, all mixed with delightful and entertaining letterpress. One of the best is "Con leading the way," where the ragamuffin on Captain de Courcey's horse is leaping a wall in splendid style.

The forty plates for "Roland Cashel" (1850) differ widely from "David Copperfield," published contemporaneously. They are too sketchy to be valuable, and the biting-in is done much more unskilfully than in many other books, "Mervyn Clitheroe," for instance. The title-page, with a strong resemblance to a plate in "Con Cregan," is well drawn ; the animals in "Brave Toro" and the "Start after luncheon" are clever, the latter having over a dozen horses drawn at full-length. The other plates are mediocre in quality, far too much dependence having been placed on the machine tint, making it appear as if "Phiz" had never entered thoroughly into the spirit of the work.

"The Daltons," completed in two volumes in 1852, contains twenty-four plates with frontispiece and an etched title-page to vol. i., and twenty-two plates to vol. ii. These again are only ordinary specimens of Browne's skill, and would show that the illustrator was reserving all his strength for the Dickens plates, which were being more carefully superintended. Some, however, are better, such as "Grounsell giving Dalton friendly advice," which is not being received very patiently; the old man in deshabille shaving being well hit off. Again "Grounsell brought to bay by the creditors of Jekyl" shows admirable study of character in the faces of the disappointed and defrauded tradespeople.

The illustration "A Hydropathic Remedy" was taken from a real incident in Lever's own experience. The writer, when English Consul at Spezzia, fell asleep in a chair at the public baths. "An English footman entering and mistaking him for the attendant, seized him by the collar, which he shook, and called for a bath. 'There,' exclaimed Lever, grasping the man of calves, and hurling him, plush and all, into the reservoir at his feet." *

The "Dodd Family abroad" (1854), with forty etched illustrations similar to the others, is written in letters from the family abroad to their Irish friends at home. As the Yankee connoisseur liked statuary better than pictures "because you can see all round," so many people like the style of literature where various aspects of the plot are given. The incidents again give ample scope for the illustrations, and the artist takes advantage of the variety to depict many varied scenes.

The four decidedly the best are "Universal Smashing," "Dodd père Marius-like sitting amidst the ruins," "Keep 'em going, or we'll be spilt," and "The first cigar:" the two latter being printed here. In the first two the text is followed closely because of the care the author takes to raise the scene to the reader's eyes, and "Phiz's" etchings take the imagination just the step farther that is needed. The third has horses galloping very like the "Two Chesnuts" in "Charles O'Malley," and "My first fall" in "David Copperfield," while the two pretty female figures in "The first cigar" are sufficiently beautiful to please the most fastidious.

"The Martins of Cro' Martin" (1856), again with forty illustrations

* "Lever's Life," vol. ii. p. 211.

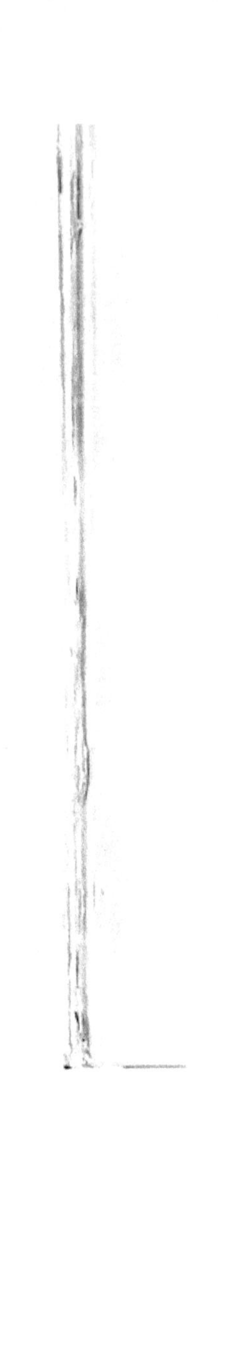

commenced in the usual monthly parts in December, 1854, and was completed in June, 1856, in twenty parts at one shilling, each part containing two etchings, 19 and 20 being, as usual, published together. Although every plate fairly reflects the text, there is a want of likeness in the series of illustrations of the chief characters, Mary Martin and Kate Henderson. Apart from this, however, the etchings were very good, the two best being " A Market-day," and "Clearing out," which present some of the finer features of Browne's Art, the former being especially characteristic.

" Old Mat's last resting-place " is a fine dramatic picture. Two fishermen are working at the grave, with Mary Martin standing alone beside it, the only mourner of her dear old friend ; the " stranger " statuesquely on top of a rock, beneath which the sea surges violently. The loneliness of the burial-place, the ruined church, and the few scattered gravestones, with the feeling throughout the picture of the strong breeze blowing inland, make the plate one of the artistic attractions of the volume.

"Davenport Dunn" appeared in the usual pink covers in twenty-two monthly shilling parts, beginning July, 1857, and ending in April, 1859. The book, said to be founded on the leading incidents of John Sadler's career, who was a junior lord of the Admiralty, is one of Lever's best, though the forty-four plates are only fair examples of the work of "Phiz." They are not all carefully drawn, but the "machined" plates have some nice figure-work and good tone of colour. The best of the illustrations are " The Pony-race," " The Man of Straw" on the title-page (which contains the germ of the whole book), "Calyper's Grotto" and " Conway on escort duty." In a note "Phiz" wrote to Mr. Robert Young, dated Banstead, Epsom, December 12, 1858, he expresses regret for keeping him waiting for one of the "Davenport Dunn " plates, which Mr. Young was engaged in biting-in with acid.

"One of Them " was begun in shilling parts in December, 1859,

A Stable Illustration.

CHAPTER VI.

THE ILLUSTRATIONS FOR AINSWORTH'S AND SMEDLEY'S WORKS.

INSWORTH'S novels contain several of the best of the "Phiz" illustrations, and it is tolerably certain that if they had been as widely read as Dickens's works, the fame of Hablôt Browne would have been considerably increased. After the careful consideration necessary for arriving at such a conclusion, it appears to me that the book which exhibits the greatest variety in Hablôt Browne's work is the now little-known but very interesting romance of "Mervyn Clitheroe," by Harrison Ainsworth. "Bleak House," which was illustrated at the same time, is very similar in character, and it may be a moot point whether it is not quite as artistically excellent as "Mervyn Clitheroe." One naturally inclines to give the more popular book the preference, but this is as much from the associations connected with the story as from the real value of the etchings. Personally I prefer the Ainsworth novel, but I should certainly not be disposed to fall out with any one who decides to put "Bleak House"

before it. But that "Mervyn Clitheroe" stands at least equal to the Dickens plates no one will, I think, deny.

"Mervyn Clitheroe" was commenced in shilling monthly parts, similar to the Dickens and Lever novels, in December, 1851, but from pressure with other undertakings it was stopped at the fourth monthly part with the announcement that "Some delay will probably occur in the continuation of the story," and that "due notice will be given of the appearance of Number V." The monthly parts — which contained thirty-two pages, with two etchings—were resumed in December, 1857, and completed in June, 1858.

The publication received considerable attention, not only because of the inherent merits of the novel, but also because of the stoppage of the story at a point where the interest in the welfare of the hero became intense. The tale is well told; it is not so lastingly popular as Charles Dickens's works, and scarcely equal to Lever's, but it is a story well worth reading, and indeed is still read in the cheap edition first published in 1879.

The novel opens in Manchester, and many incidents are from Ainsworth's own experience of school-life there. The main mystery of the story is the disappearance of the will made by Mervyn's Uncle Mobberly, who had brought up the hero and led him to believe he would be the inheritor of his wealth. But when the will is read he is found not to be the heir. As usual, however, virtue is triumphant in the end; Mervyn obtains his rights, marries a titled lady and "lives happily ever afterwards."

The plates were executed in Browne's two methods of work, some being etching pure and simple, and others being the combination of etching and machine engraving, which in his hands has frequently given such excellent results. The frontispiece, where Phaley is striking Ned Culcheth, with Lupus and Gaunt, the dogs, leaping on the gipsy, is one of the finest plates "Phiz" produced. It is a brilliant picture, grandly composed and splendidly drawn—a perfect realisation of the text, and a beautiful study of sea and moonlight in black and white. In the early edition this was printed with lovely ink, which by time has become slightly sepia-coloured, and some magnificent impressions are occasionally to be found. The plate is now rather worn, otherwise I should have introduced it here.

" My Uncle Mobberly's Will is read," is the very opposite of the dark and mysterious frontispiece. Here all is definition—and clear definition—of character, with a touch of humour very pleasing to examine. The old lawyer reading the will which for the time deprives Mervyn of his inheritance, and the various expressions of attention, expectation, disappointment and chagrin, complacency and triumph, are quite as well represented as in the larger and more laborious but not more successful "Reading the Will" by Sir David Wilkie.

The original drawing for "My Uncle Mobberly's Will" is in the collection of the Duchess of St. Albans. It was my intention to have reproduced the drawing here to compare with the finished plate, but many of the lines have been found too faint to print so as to show the extreme delicacy of the pencil work. The plate, however, is almost a literal copy from it, and retains nearly all the best qualities of the first idea, though it is to be feared the number of impressions taken from the steel has caused some of the weaker parts to show signs of wearing.

As a contrast to this, the plate of the " Meeting in Delamere Forest " is also printed here : a fine effect obtained by machine work and skill in printing. The steel appears to be hard, as it is scarcely worn at all, and the impressions in this book are as perfect as those in the first copies. In the " Will-reading " the etching is almost all pure line work, with no more colour than absolutely necessary, while in the other exactly the reverse is the case—there is scarcely a line to be seen in it, and it is as full of rich luminous colour as a plate can be charged.

Amongst Mr. Young's collection of letters there is one from Ainsworth to Hablôt Browne, dated February 14th, 1858, in which one of the illustrations to " Mervyn Clitheroe " is mentioned, and where the author expresses his

satisfaction with the illustrations, though the publishers—unreasonably enough —appear to have been grumbling.   It says :—

"MY DEAR BROWNE,—I have received the enclosed note from Mr. Warne, of the firm of Routledge & Co.

"I have answered to say that the subject of the second plate was sent to you on Thursday.

"I did not perceive that the *best* plates were hurried, as Mr. Warne seems to intimate.   They came out extremely well, I think, and are generally liked.

"I hope the present subject will suit you.   'The Conjurors Interrupted' will be effective, if I am not mistaken.

"Pray tell your plate-printer to send me proofs early (no matter how rough), that I may prevent any variations between the text and the illustrations.   And be as early as you conveniently can, in order to prevent any grumbling on the part of Mr. Warne.   I suppose he will require to publish on Thursday, 25th.—Yours always, W. HARRISON AINSWORTH."

In "Old St. Paul's" (1847), the only two plates signed "Phiz" are the frontispiece and the vignette, both of which are excellent illustrations. The first is the "Song of the Plague," where the undertakers make merry in their warehouse: "their seats were coffins and their table was a coffin set upon a bier."   The other is "The Piper in the Dead-cart," an incident in the Plague, where a piper taken for dead recovers his senses to find himself being carried to the burial-place.   He takes heart and sets to work to play his pipes, which so terrifies the drivers that they make off from their dismal conveyance.   The architectural portion of the plate is clever.   The remaining illustrations by another etcher do not add much to the value of the book.

The eighteen plates which illustrate Ainsworth's "Crichton" are all very carefully drawn and finished, presenting the romance of the "admirable" youth in scenes of sixteenth-century life full of variety.   "The Venice Glass" plate shows Crichton discovering that the Queen has conspired to poison him, the incident being treated very dramatically.   The "Descent of the Column" is exciting, though it loses a great deal by not showing the hand above cutting the rope, as Franklin did in his cartoons for the same novel.

In " Auriol," a madman-like story of the elixir of life, " Phiz " is not

Hugh Paytings and the Chaplain.   From "The Spendthrift."

so interesting.   The best plates are the " Elixir of Long Life," and the

" Hand and the Cloak;" while the weird broken-down house in Vauxhall Road has a fascination about it which is very powerful, and the plate has been styled Rembrandtesque in its effect. "Crichton" and "Auriol" were both first published in Ainsworth's magazine, the title given to the latter being there " Revelations of London."

The change in the style of "Phiz's" work becomes evident in the woodcut illustrations to " The Spendthrift " (1857), and " Ovingdean Grange " (1860). In the first, some of the eight cuts are fairly good and maintain the artist's reputation for insight of character and rapid realisation of it; but in the other —three years later, it will be observed—signs of decline become more manifest, and the first steps on the downward path show themselves distinctly. The cut used here, " Hugh Paynings and the Chaplain," is one of the best of " The Spendthrift " series. In " Ovingdean Grange," the eight cuts are not of the best class, as the illustrator has not succeeded in seizing the chief characteristics either of the Roundheads or of the Cavaliers. All Ainsworth's novels were republished in a smaller size in 1879, each volume containing six illustrations.

Like the Lever illustrations, the drawings made for Ainsworth's books have become scattered, some being still in the family, while others have been sold in small numbers to various collectors.

It is, perhaps, worth noting as eminently characteristic of the men, that in the only published memoir of Harrison Ainsworth, George Cruikshank figures largely and Browne is never mentioned. Cruikshank was always well able to keep himself before the public—as he was quite legitimately entitled to do— but Hablòt Browne was altogether too shy to push himself forward, and the result of this is seen in the extraordinary omission of even a mention of Browne in the memoir. Browne's work for Ainsworth's novels is certainly better than Cruikshank's, and as has been said, " Phiz " never did a more successful series of plates than those for " Mervyn Clitheroe:" yet Ainsworth's biographer cannot even vouchsafe him a passing notice.

HEN Frank Smedley's first book was published—the celebrated "Frank Fairlegh"—it was illustrated by George Cruikshank; but three of his other works had plates by "Phiz;" namely, "Lewis Arundel," "Harry Coverdale," and "The Colville Family."

"Lewis Arundel" was published in 1852, with forty-two etchings by "Phiz." These are just a little mannered in their style, and are not so good as those the artist was doing at the same time for other books, but they were still good work of such a kind as he had no need to be ashamed. The dog, Faust, which plays a prominent part in the story, is always well-drawn, but Lewis himself is never quite satisfactorily represented. The etching, "Meeting a very trying Relative," is clever: the scientist with thoughts in the clouds, and paying little heed to the outward man, meets Leicester with other two dandies, and, much to Leicester's annoyance, stops to speak to him. The pathos and poetry in the "Three Steps in Life" is refined and delicate; but the theatrical attitude of "Falling in and falling out" is absurd. "A False Start," is a subject after Browne's own heart, with all the incidents of the beginning of a run duly depicted, though the rocking-horse-looking animal in front is stupid enough.

"The Fortunes of the Colville Family" (1853), contains a frontispiece and a vignette on the title by "Phiz," of not more than ordinary merit. The angel forms on the vignette are, however, beautifully drawn, the good angels being in light and the evil ones in shade.

"Harry Coverdale's Courtship," with twenty-nine plates, which was published in fifteen one-shilling parts in 1854, contains a number of cleverly drawn running horses; "Spitting a Spy," "A Foul Stroke," and "A Fencing Lesson," being the chief. The best plate in the book and the best done for Smedley's novels is the one printed here, "Getting up the Steam," where

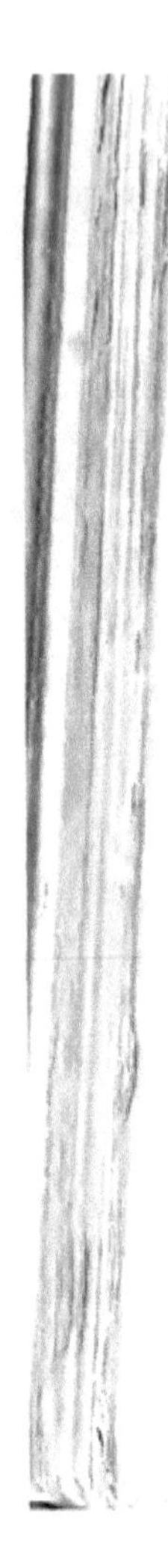

" Don Whiskerandos," the attendant of Countess Nasimoff, and a hotel commissionaire fall out about the luggage, and "grimace and chatter in a polygot jargon apparently compounded of every language under heaven, and utterly incomprehensible to the deepest philologist extant."

By the courtesy of Messrs. Virtue & Co. I have learned from their books that the drawing of the design for the wrapper of the parts of "Lewis Arundel" was executed on November 7th, 1850, £8 8s. being paid for it. For each etching "Phiz" received £8 18s. 6d., and the same price was maintained for the "Harry Coverdale" plates, which were completed in December, 1855.

An Old Stager

Fac-simile of the first known sketch by "Phiz." Lent by Mr. F. G. Kitton

CHAPTER VII.

HABLÔT BROWNE AS A COLOURIST.   HIS WATER-COLOUR DRAWINGS.

ALTHOUGH I freely admit that "Phiz" is only to be thoroughly admired in his pencil-drawings for illustrations, and in the etched plates for the same, yet as he did some remarkable work in water-colour drawings as well as in oil paintings, I think the examples he has left in both mediums well worthy of serious consideration, and certainly deserving of more attention than they had received before his death.

Browne exhibited in his early days at the Royal Academy and the Free Exhibition at Hyde Park Corner, as well as at the British Institution and

Society of British Artists in later times; but his name has never been popularly connected with any art but that of illustration. It was not until the two exhibitions of his works took place, first in Liverpool, afterwards in London, that it was generally recognised he had some talent for pictorial art of a larger kind than could be bound up in a volume.

This discovery of Browne's capacity to paint — so to term what was known to the artist's personal friends — is very similar to the result of the Bewick exhibition three years before the "Phiz" collection was gathered together. As I mention in my "Life of Bewick," little or no notice had previously been taken of that artist's work in colour, and the admirers of his designs in black and white were, as a rule, astonished to see the delicate and refined colour of his minute sketches. Some, indeed, maintained that the best of these drawings were not Bewick's at all, evidently being unable to believe that the artist in monochrome could be so great a genius in varied tints.

Hablôt Browne, though similar in this one respect, yet differs widely from Bewick in regard to the relation between his paintings and his other work. In Bewick's case the most cultured can admire the lovely tinting in the vignettes and birds, and never cease to feel satisfied with and praise his exquisite productions. But with Browne's labours in colour we dare not be so enthusiastic. It is always pleasant to be able to praise the works of those artists whom, for other reasons, we admire—to try to find beauties in all their achievements. But as we are forced to admit that Reynolds failed in purely ideal paintings, that Turner never was very certain in his figure drawing, and that Doré's anatomy was faulty and technique poor, so we feel it to be unwise as well as incorrect to claim for Browne exceptional merit in his coloured productions. "Phiz" was a genius and a great artist without his paintings, yet while I wish to point out their excellencies and beauties, I wish the reader to understand that in this department he is not claimed to be a great master.

The gift of colour, it should be remembered, requires careful and assiduous cultivation, so that the man who spent the greater portion of his life in drawing in black and white could scarcely be expected to attain to that perfection which constant practice almost alone can give.

Any one without knowledge of Browne's art who is shown the drawing belonging to the Hon. H. Romilly, styled simply "A Landscape," and almost any of Browne's larger water-colour sketches of figures, would hesitate to declare them to be the work of the same hand. They seem to exhibit not the usual variance of different periods of labour, or the natural inequality of human temperament, but rather the execution of different brains and hands.

Mr. Romilly's drawing is only a small sketch, in water-colours, of a scene amidst the Welsh or Cumberland hills. Trees in autumnal tints nearly fill the foreground, and the distant mountains are enveloped in an atmosphere which assumes a brilliant and natural deep ultramarine in the valley at the base. Contrast this with many of the figure subjects and all the Heads which Browne produced at different times. The Heads are almost invariably poor, inaccurately drawn and badly coloured. He never seems to have been able to make a really artistic and powerful drawing of a head larger than for an illustration, and even in those it is only now and again that he thoroughly succeeded.

It is impossible to name all the water-colour drawings which Browne executed of which a word of praise might fitly be recorded. There were fully two hundred examples at Liverpool in 1883, and a number of others were in the London exhibition later in the year, and a critical estimate of only a few of the very best need be given in this chapter, as the next chapter deals with the chief drawings done specially with a view to illustration. One of the water-colours belonging to Dr. Edgar Browne, called "Fifty miles from anywhere," is a worthy successor to Mr. Romilly's landscape. It represents a view half-way up a mountain-side; the colour is low in tone but true to nature, and very delightful in feeling. Another of Mr. Romilly's drawings,

"Surrey," is about the same size as this, but is of a different character. The warm glow of the foreground is in fine harmony with the russets and graduated blue-greys farther off. Some care has been taken with this drawing, as the distance has been washed again and again to obtain atmosphere, and this gives the drawing a value which many of his drawings do not possess. "Where are we now?" shows a man standing holding the reins

Fac-simile of the last drawing by "Phiz." Lent by Mr. G. Halse.

of his horse on top of a ridge of hill which overlooks a lengthy level country, with just the faintest indications of a city in mid-distance. The colour is by no means brilliant, yet it is in good harmony, and something between the warmth of "Surrey" and the coolness of "Fifty miles from anywhere." "Giving John a warming," a large drawing (about 20 inches by 16 inches) is one of the most carefully finished. Three young ladies of the fashion of 1860 are riding hard across country, followed as fast as possible by "Old

John," who is considerably put about by the speed at which duty compels
him to proceed. The movement of the horses is admirable, and the colour is
as good as can be wished in such a subject. "The Legitimate Drama in the
Provinces" is the title of a drawing now in the possession of Mr. David
MacBrayne, of Glasgow, having been presented to him by Mr. R. Young.
Opposite the chief inn of the village Punch has set up his theatre. Rusties
and children stand around, with a sturdy housewife in the front, and a farmer
on horseback at the rear. One of the children hides his face in his mother's
lap as Punch shrieks and jumps forward.

The headpiece to this chapter is the earliest identified sketch by "Phiz,"
probably done before 1830. The print on the previous page is the very last
drawing he is known to have executed. The first is in the collection of Mr.
F. G. Kitton, and the other in that of Mr. G. Halse. Neither of them are
sufficiently important to require serious criticism, but the laboured feeling of
the former and the freedom of the latter indicate the immense practice the
artist obtained in the interval between.

I won my Wife on horseback.   From "Flood and Field."

CHAPTER VIII.

OTHER WATER-COLOUR AND PENCIL DRAWINGS, CHIEFLY FOR ILLUSTRATIONS.

BESIDES the water-colour drawings mentioned in the previous chapter, which Hablôt Browne executed as pictures or as sketches without special design for illustrations, there are a large number existing which were made for publication, sooner or later, after translation into slight tint or into black and white. A great portion of these having been exhibited in the Liverpool Exhibition, I have taken the numbers of that collection for such as were then shown, and made notes on the designs in the order in which they were hung. It is

R

unnecessary to mention more than the representative drawings, and where
possible an indication of the time of production is added. Many of these
drawings were also in the London Exhibition.

Some of these works were drawn in sets, and one of the largest and
best is that illustrating Shakespeare's "Venus and Adonis." There were
one hundred different designs, drawn in groups of five (Nos. 59 to 78,
Liverpool Exhibition), having a large circular drawing in the centre and
four small ones surrounding it and filling up the corners. They have not
yet been published, but may some day appear, as, though unequal, like all
Browne's work, they contain much that would make them acceptable to the
public. They are more free adaptations from the text than exact illustrations, and are thus more representative of the artist's imagination than the
poet's feelings.

"Death's Revel" (233) and "Death's Banquet" (239), both the property of Dr. Edgar Browne, were probably intended to be published
separately as prints. The first is one of the finest sombre designs "Phiz"
ever did, and quite equal in conception to his large oil paintings. Death
is being dealt to all people by all kinds of instruments which can stab or
beat down. At one place a child is just about to be stabbed when the
mother clutches the knife and a deadly struggle goes on for the mastery.
At another, one man has murdered another and is just raising himself as a
miscreant lances him; in turn another man is dealing a tremendous blow
with a tomahawk at the last-mentioned. In the background a horseman
wages deadly warfare with a man on foot; and above and beyond Death
holds out his hands, as if accepting all who are thus entering his domain.
The companion drawing, "Death's Banquet," is not quite so fine. Every
one is dead here, and the scene is evidently intended to represent the end
of the struggles of the "Revel." Birds of prey are beginning to swoop
down on the dead men, women, and horses, and Death above all drinks out
of a skull to the success of his mission. Both these drawings are executed

with pencil, ink, and tint, and are on grey-toned paper, which greatly helps the effect.

Another series of drawings, as yet unpublished, is the set of twelve which illustrate Wordsworth's "Hartleap Well" (390-4). These are very spirited drawings, and quite worthy of the best period of "Phiz's" labours. Another series gives sketches (110) for the "Stolen Heart," where the various vicissitudes a lover's heart is supposed to go through are hit off in six clever tableaux. "How Pippins enjoyed a day with the foxhounds" (336) and "Dame Perkins's ride to market" (337), the first with twelve designs and the other with ten, have both been published as hunting-sketches, which met with a ready sale. They represent the serious adventures of Pippins in his unaccustomed following of the hounds; and Dame Perkins's trouble with her grey mare, which will persist in keeping up with the field, to the old lady's present dismay but ultimate triumph, as she is first in at the death and is presented with the brush as the heroine. These drawings are beautifully finished and well drawn, the characters being carefully preserved throughout.

Browne appears to have felt keenly one of the greatest disadvantages of pictorial Art—the difficulty of representing a sequence of events. He never was quite satisfied with one drawing of a subject, but frequently drew the same figures in a different position, thus carrying on the story by stages; and all the preceding were in this manner.

Browne also made a series of drawings representative of the various minor plagues of life, as "Wind" (12), "Fog" (13), "Dust" (14), "Snow" (17), and "Fire" (228), where the characteristics of each are easily recognisable. "Sic transit" is a cartoon with representations of the five ages of woman, delicately drawn and with more than usual care. "Acis and Galatea" (177-179) is another series in a similar style and very well finished.

"Phiz" executed a considerable number of drawings after the style of Leech's well-known large coloured sketches, as well as many smaller works in colour which were afterwards employed as illustrations. Some of these are far from successful, the least satisfactory of all being a large number of designs for statuettes and clock ornaments, which are neither beautiful in themselves nor practicable to work from.

A series of drawings of Irish scenes executed by " Phiz " in 1847 has often been the subject of remark in the brief notices of the artist which have appeared in print. There is a certain air of mystery about this series which excites the interest and leads to a wish to know exactly what these drawings are and what they were intended to be. All that has hitherto been known is that a number of more than usually excellent Irish drawings in crayons existed, but the intention of the artist in their preparation seems never to have been divulged.

The drawings were executed (as mentioned in the " Memoir ") in October, 1847, after a journey through the poorest districts in Ireland, at the time of the great potato famine. Browne made many small sketches of such subjects as struck him, and from these, on his return to England, he composed large drawings of the Irish peasantry. The series thus executed numbered at least a score of works of about twenty-four inches by sixteen, which rank as the finest of the artist's productions in this method of work. They are now scattered, but a number were gathered together at the two " Phiz " exhibitions, and formed an important and attractive part of the collections. The family still retain several, and Mr. W. J. Spooner, Mr. R. Hampson, and Mr. Frederick Wigan are also owners of fine examples from the series.

The drawings were executed as preliminary studies for etchings, and six plates were commenced but never completed. These plates are in such a condition that they could still be printed from, and as they are most elaborate subjects and very carefully drawn there is some likelihood that impressions will be offered for sale. No better specimen of the artist's work could be obtained.

From unpublished Drawing for " The Riddle of Ivy Green." Lent by Mr. G. Halse.

HROUGHOUT this volume there are scattered numerous little sketches by " Phiz," as well as illustrated letters and notes, which would make a lengthy list if separately named. They were the outcome of Hablôt Browne's overflowing genius at various times in his life, though the majority were probably executed between 1850 and 1860. Besides these, the family have a very large number of sketches still unsold, some of them of the very highest quality, and varied in their subjects. Some of the large sketches " Phiz " etched from his notes when in Ireland are also among Dr. Browne's collection. These Irish sketches were drawn on paper of a large size, after the expedition to Ireland already referred to. Many of them have found honoured places in collections of drawings, but it is to be feared that in other cases the value of the works is unrecognised by their owners. Those in Dr. Browne's possession are a little smaller than others, but are large enough (about sixteen by twelve) to allow of great freedom of that touch and breadth of handling the crayon which are characteristic of this series of drawings.

Towards the end of 1880 Browne executed a set of twenty-four drawings, in pencil and sepia, for Mr. George Halse. These Mr. Halse intended to use as illustrations for one of his stories, " Lot 94," afterwards incorporated with others in the " Salad of Stray Leaves," but the idea of separate publication being abandoned, the drawings have never appeared. For " The Riddle of Ivy Green," another story in the " Salad of Stray Leaves," " Phiz " did twelve drawings, and these also are unpublished. Two of them are introduced into this and the previous pages, and for the use of them I have to thank Mr. Halse, in whose possession the whole series remains.

The last drawing Browne did for illustration was for the frontispiece of Mr. Halse's "Salad of Stray Leaves," an entertaining book of short stories. This drawing is here reproduced, and a little difference will be found between it and the wood engraving, which Browne slightly altered in the block. This drawing was done by the artist in 1882, the year of his death, when his hand had so far lost its power that he could use his three middle fingers only, the thumb being paralyzed. In order to make the designs appear with some detail when reduced, Browne was compelled to execute them on a large scale, as he could not then draw minutely. Hence the want of artistic feeling in the lines, so different from the earlier work of the illustrator, and one which cannot too deeply be deplored.

From unpublished Drawing for " The Riddle of Ivy Green."
Lent by Mr. G. Halse.

THE GENIUS OF "PHIZ" EXEMPLIFIED.

CHAPTER IX.

OIL PAINTINGS.

I T is one of the most trying tasks of the biographer who desires to give the subject of his labours the utmost honour possible, to be compelled to admit that his hero did not always excel in the paths he wished to tread, so as to obtain admiration as well as ultimate renown. It would be a ludicrous error for a writer to prepare a volume on the Life and Labours of any one whom he could not honestly and thoroughly admire, and it is therefore not easy for such a one to admit thorough failure in one branch of his subject's life-work wherein he himself thought he excelled.

I think it will be allowed that enough admiration has been expressed for the genuine triumphs of Hablôt Browne's Art to counterbalance any feeling of disappointment which may be felt when the unwilling verdict is pronounced that Browne's labours in oil painting cannot be placed on the same level as the successful illustrations by " Phiz."

I do not say that Browne thoroughly failed as an oil painter—no one could say that who has seen his finest works in that medium—but I think it must frankly be admitted that he did not excel as an exponent of the art of painting in oil colours, and that no one can seriously study his pictures as works worthy of imitation, from which may be gathered lessons likely to help forward the well-being of Art. Hablôt Browne, technically speaking, did not paint at all. He only coloured his designs, much in the way he often tinted his water-colour drawings. He was not able so to manipulate his colours that the painter, as a workman and connoisseur in methods of production, can admire his manner of work, or "technique," as the expression is. Broadly speaking, an artist will pardon a picture which is a poor subject treated with careless composition and loose drawing if the "technique," or way the paint is laid on the canvas, is good. But though the subject be worthy of thought, the composition all that can be required, and the drawing careful and beautiful, let the "technique" be poor and uncultivated, and artists—at least, those of the present day—will regard the picture as something to be almost despised.

To judge Hablôt Browne's oil paintings from a technical point of view is at once to appreciate their weakness as painted works, though his reputation for conception and composition suffers not at all. In the most ambitious of his paintings—in respect that it is his largest and one that received very careful attention—"Les Trois Vifs et les Trois Morts," the composition is well carried out, the parts balancing each other with true pictorial effect; the drawing is fair and the story well told. Had a technically-trained painter executed it the picture would probably have ranked with the best in the decade; but because of the lack of technical knowledge on the designer's part, the picture fails to impress the spectator. It is evident at a glance that the colour is crude and almost ignorantly applied, the "quality" is *nil*, and, to the modern student, the whole is more an example of what ought to be avoided in oil painting than of what may be admired.

The reason for this failure on Hablôt Browne's part is easily discerned.

He had no training in the mechanical difficulties of the Art. What no teacher can supply, *le vif génie*, he had in plenty, but of what the most elementary teacher could have shown him he seems to have been ignorant. Unfortunately he gloried in his ignorance, and thus missed entering the ranks of artists of the noblest class. Gustave Doré, too, it will be remembered, erred in the same way; he, like Hablôt Browne, had great power of conception, yet he quite failed to properly carry out his ideas because of his bad technique, and also because his drawing was wretched. Here certainly Browne had a distinct advantage over the painter of "Moses and the Serpents" or "Christ leaving the Prætorium," for his drawing was usually correct and only occasionally wrong, while Doré's drawing was seldom right, and often far and lamentably wrong.

The most carefully finished of Hablôt Browne's larger oil pictures is "Sintram and Death descending into the Dark Valley." This is not nearly so large as the "Three Living and Three Dead," but is a more concentrated and better finished painting. Preceded by Death riding on a pale horse, and holding high an hour-glass, Sintram rides fearlessly on his chesnut charger, carrying at the end of his lance the head of a monster pierced through. Down into the deep dark valley they go, and we seem to obtain a foretaste of the horrors contained therein by the suggestive reptiles seen here and there at the entrance. The imagination begins to be fevered, and the trunks of the trees take unusual and dreadful shapes. Faces hideous and grinning are visible at every turn of the much-twisted branches, and the dog accompanying the traveller unwillingly follows with tail between his legs. What mars the painting is the amateurish style of the workmanship, as well as a crude red spot placed on the saddle, which greatly damages the harmony of the picture, and, to my mind, utterly spoils the whole charm of the otherwise excellent work. A clever pencil first-thought of this picture is in Dr. Browne's possession.

Hablôt Browne's largest picture, as has already been mentioned, is "Les

s

Trois Vifs et les Trois Morts," a canvas which attracted much attention both at the Liverpool and the London exhibitions of the artist's works. An armoured knight, a page, and an old almoner, all on horseback, have just emerged from a wood. Riding briskly along they are suddenly confronted with horsemen on pale steeds, whose sides are hollow, the ribs appearing to the eye. Each rider is seen to be a skeleton, and the three living men draw up as they hear the fateful words spoken :—

> "Looke! suche as we are, suche shall ye be,
> And suche as we were, such be ye!"

Each skeleton represents the age of the three living horsemen, and beckons to his similitude with threatening look and gesture. In the picture there are also five dogs, panic-stricken with the terrorising sight, crouching down full of fear.

The work of the painting—which is about eight feet long—is extremely thin. There appears to have been first a ground of brown (let us hope it is not asphaltum), and on this the picture, at least the lower portion of it, is painted. One of the dogs in the foreground is simply touched in with a dark brown colour, with a little white for light, and the general body of the animal is of the bituminous underground—a kind of work which is clever, but scarcely admissible in ordinarily finished work.* There is little or no attempt at technical excellence, and the work is like a scene-painter's, who knows his effect must be broad to appear well at a distance. There are some patches of brilliant red on the old man's cape, the knight's horse's nose, and the strap of the youth's horse and dagger-hilt, which are very objectionable from an artistic point of view. They perhaps assist in giving brightness to the picture, but the crudity of the pure vermilion can never be forgiven.

This picture, like all Browne's other work, was produced without direct

---

* Students of the Louvre pictures will, however, remember that a distinguished impressionist, and one who could not be accused of want of "technique" in his work, often painted in the same way. Theodore Rousseau in his masterpiece, "Le Coucher du Soleil," represents a large foreground stone in a similar manner.

reference to models; it was probably drawn small and then enlarged. It was completed only a very short time before a serious paralytic affliction overtook him, and it may thus be put down as the crowning effort of his genius in oil painting. It is a good picture, and, except for the single fault mentioned, lack of technical excellence, would be thoroughly fine.

A set of four sporting pictures belonging to Mrs. Westall, the widow of Browne's family doctor, are all better in tone than either of the two paintings just described. There are two of shooting, and one each of hunting and fishing. In the first, the one with the boy laughing at his master missing a bird, the sky and general tone of distance are particularly fine, a pearly grey with many subtle half tints being artistically used.

Mrs. Westall's "Market-day in Ireland" is rather disjointed, each group seemingly separated from the other. Each group is good alone, but together they make a poor composition. But the landscape is particularly fine, the sky and the foreground (where blackberries trail over some rocks) being also an excellent transcript from nature.

Another picture, the property of Dr. Vincent Ambler, "Used up," is one that bears a strong likeness to Thomas Bewick's experimental woodcut design, "Waiting for Death," being similar in feeling and in moral. An old horse crawling along a road is being barked at by three dogs. In the distance is an old Rhenish castle; nearer is a toll-house and bar, and everything about them is "used up." Beyond a vision is given of a new life springing up. Many chimneys indicating industry, smoke from out the ruins of a once-famous monastery, and a steamer, tell further of the newer existence which seems to have little in common with the older. The whole picture is symbolical of the death of feudal and priestridden times, the old horse which once did good work being yelped at through the assurance of a generation which knoweth not Joseph. The whole feeling of the picture is strongly Bewickian in its design, and the unsatisfactoriness of the painting is almost forgotten in the interest of the subject.

Another painting is called "The Toll-bar." A straw rope is laid across the road by some children as the Squire approaches. One of the youngsters laughingly, yet shyly, touches his forelock as if appealing for the toll, which, of course, will be presently given. This is painted with broad scenic effect, but somewhat coarsely, though the sky, trees, and distance are very fair. Another large but very unpleasant work is a young man's dream in delirium tremens ; dice, cards, drink, lust, horror, fear, malice, revenge, spite, murder, greed, hate, and every evil thing appear as thrilling through his disordered brain.

In all there were twenty-four oil pictures shown at Liverpool, and these included all the exhibited oil paintings in the London collection, so that this may be taken as representing nearly all the larger works in oil completed by Hablôt Browne.

Petrified with horror. From "Flood and Field."

CHAPTER X.

TOGETHER with the volumes already enumerated which contain engravings by Browne, there were a large number of miscellaneous books illustrated by him, some of them with plates of very fine quality. A list embracing nearly all the volumes embellished by "Phiz" is given in the Appendix; but as many of the engravings deserve special attention, the chief works are treated in more detail in the following notes.

In our Memoir of the artist reference is made to Winkles' "Cathedral Churches" as being amongst the earliest published works of Hablôt Browne along with the "historical" John Gilpin. The first volume appeared complete in 1836, the second in 1838, and the third in 1842. For the latter Browne did nothing, but for the first volume twenty-six of the views were drawn in outline or etched on the steel plate by him, and eleven were done for the second. The book was published in monthly parts, commencing in 1835, some time before the " Pickwick " plates were begun. The plates show careful attention to the drawing, and display an intimacy with and mastery over the intricacies of architecture rather unexpected from the creator of the pictorial Sam Weller or David Copperfield. The only visible link of connection is that now and then the little figures introduced in the cathedral views are caricatured ; for instance, in the undercroft of Canterbury the guide showing the crypt is a fat podgy figure and the visitor is a long and lanky man—quite a comical contrast to each other. " St. Paul's from Southwark " is a beautiful plate, and the best in the series. To Winkles, the engraver, credit must be given for the lovely light and shade, but it is to Browne that we owe the charming arrangement of forms, the majesty of the distant church, and the skilfully placed figures in the front plan. The plates of " Salisbury, West Front," " Wells Cathedral, West Front," and " Winchester Cathedral," looking across the nave, are also excellent examples of conscientious youthful labour.

In 1838, after the pronounced success of " Pickwick," " Jorrocks's Jaunts and Jollities " was published, with twelve etchings by " Phiz," a name then much better known than the artist's own. These designs are perhaps an improvement on the " Pickwick " plates, and in two instances are very fine specimens of the illustrator's work. " The Meet," though rather inclined to caricature, has many well-drawn horses and dogs, the tiny figures in the distance being cleverly inserted. The other, representing Jorrocks riding through the fog with a mailcoach lamp strapped to his back, in order to pierce the thick atmosphere, is a delightfully fine piece of etching work.

Chatto's clever little book on " Tobacco " (1839), for which he assumed the *nom de plume* of Joseph Fume, is illustrated by half-a-dozen good etchings. One of the plates bearing two of these etchings is here introduced, and gives the old vicar and the English labourer, both enjoying the sanctified use of the pipe. The latter, which gives the " hardworking

labourer smoking by the side of his hearth at night, and presenting a perfect picture of quiet enjoyment," is not nearly so good as the other, which is thus noticed in Chatto's work :—

" The old vicar, restored to his old parsonage, enjoyed a pipe when seated in his armchair, pondering on the subject of his next Sunday's sermon, with a jug of sound old ale and a huge tome of sound old divinity on the table before him, for the occasional refreshment as well of the bodily as the spiritual man."

Seven plates illustrating Robertson's three-volume novel of " Solomon Seesaw " (1839) are a good deal in the style of the " Pickwick " etchings. The figures, however appropriate to the story, are a little caricatured, the best being " The Marshalsea Election " and " Dr. Robbin's Smoking-room."

In 1841 " Phiz " did some unequal work, and the plates in Neale's novel of " Paul Periwinkle; or, the Pressgang," are as excellent as the illustrations for " Pelham's Chronicles of Crime " are poor. In the former the best plate is " The Night Surprise," with two highwaymen chasing Dick Doubtful. The three horsemen are flying along the road at the highest speed, but the part of the design not strictly illustrative is the best artistically. The background with a direction-post, a windmill, fine rich foliage, and a glorious sky make up as complete a picture as " Phiz " had done up to this time. " The Prosperity going down," " The Collision with the Prosperity," " The Heroine's Escape," and " Mr. Wrynecker enjoying a beautiful morning," are all etchings of the best class. The fifty-two plates prepared for " Pelham's Chronicles of Crime " (1841) bear evidence of having been executed more as contributors to the family funds than as work done to increase reputation and extend fame. The two which rise above the level of ordinary illustration are " Witchery at Woodstock " and " A Meeting of Witches," and this betterness is because of the humour introduced into subjects where it is perfectly permissible. It is not, however, either permissible or desirable to introduce anything the least caricatured

into such scenes of evil as most of these plates illustrate. At this time
"Phiz" seemed to have been incapable of conceiving his subjects with
proper gravity, and it was not until a few years later, in "The Dark Road" of
"Dombey and Son" (see page 124) and kindred etchings, that he found a
higher art than the caricaturist's. In "Pelham's Chronicles of Crime" there
are illustrations of "Oxford shooting the Queen" and the "Assassination of
Perceval" which are quite unworthy of the reality. They serve better than
anything else to show by comparison with later works the progress Browne
made in the higher art of the representation of true seriousness. Twelve
plates illustrating Mrs. Trollope's three-volume novel of "Charles Chester-
field" (1841), are superior to those in the "Chronicles of Crime," and have
little of that feeling of caricature which so hurts the etchings in the
last-named book.

"Godfrey Malvern," by G. T. Miller (1842), contains in two volumes
twenty-six etchings by "Phiz," all of which are fairly successful. "Gregory
Gruff and the Widow" and the succeeding illustration of the same pair are
full of legitimate humour and knowledge of character. "Godfrey's Interview
with the Publisher" is also fine and much better than the similar and
contemporary illustration for "Nicholas Nickleby." The young author's
figure is, for "Phiz," unusually well drawn. "Love and Remorse" and
"Love and Death" are also excellent.

In Maxwell's "Rambling Recollections of a Soldier of Fortune," 1842
(afterwards published as "Flood and Field" in 1857), there are two spirited
woodcuts, which are both printed here (by Messrs. Routledge's permission),
one at page 189, and the other as a headpiece to this chapter. The first, "I
won my Wife on horseback" is an illustration to the story of a youth who by
a brilliant "big leap" over a tremendous fence so gained the admiration
and affection of an heiress that next morning the pair eloped to Gretna
Green. The second represents "Mr. McDermott checkmated," the hero of
another tale, who having run off from a rich but vulgar woman he had

married, is now discovered, by his newly wedded partner, through the cleverness of her servant Tony, and becomes "Petrified with horror:"—

"I, in the innocency of my heart, dreamed not of the surprise in preparation and, wrapped in my dressing-gown, was drowning easy thoughts over a trial for murder in *The Herald*, and between the production of fresh witnesses was quietly sipping my tea. The door opened; no doubt 'the maid-of-all-work' with a fresh muffin. A pair of lusty arms enfolded me. I looked up—my 'bonny bride' had locked me closely in her embrace. Behind, the villain Tony was standing, keeping the door ajar to secure a retreat."

Carleton's "Traits and Stories of the Irish Peasantry," of 1843, contains twenty-two etchings in volume i. and fourteen in volume ii., by various artists. In volume i. six are by "Phiz" and there are three in volume ii. None of these are very good, and they resemble Ainsworth's "Auriol" in the poverty of their colour. The number for March of the same year of the *New Sporting Magazine* contains a melody, "The Rare Old British Worthy," with six fine plates by "Phiz." Three of these plates were printed separately from the text in the usual way; but the other three have been printed after or before the letterpress, and it is somewhat difficult without careful examination to tell whether they are woodcuts or etchings.

There is a curious and uncommon connection between the novel "Samuel Sowerby," published in London in 1843, and "The Commissioner," published in Dublin in the same year. The latter possesses twenty-eight plates, and "Samuel Sowerby" is embellished with twenty of the same plates, but with different titles and arranged in other sequences. The most ridiculous passages have had to be inserted in the "Sowerby" to make the illustrations agree with the text, and the whole novel (which otherwise is very well) bears the impress of having been "written up" to the plates. As an instance of what has been done we may take the plate called in "The Commissioner" "Joel's walk down the Strand," where a young man in women's clothes is being addressed by a stranger. In "Samuel Sowerby" this identical plate is inserted, but the title on the plate has been effaced and a new title written. "The Recognition" is now its name; the text describes the incident as being "Sir Flipperton Fairfax and his paramour walking down the Strand at ten in the morning." It ought to be said, however, that the reader who never saw the plates under other titles might be quite satisfied with them in either volume.

Other two books of 1845 are Rodwell's "Memoirs of an Umbrella," illustrated with sixty-eight clever cuts by "Phiz," and the memoirs of R. W. Elliston, the comedian, which were began in 1844, with illustrations by G. Cruikshank. The continuation appeared in 1845, with two plates by "Phiz," "Tangent at Home," and "A Falling Star," both of them clever.

In 1846 a small pamphlet of thirty-four pages was published, with five exceptionally fine and characteristic plates by "Phiz." The "Dissection of Teetotalism" was the title given to it, it being an attack on the teetotal movement and a defence of the worshippers of Bacchus. The illustrations represent some of the terrible results likely to happen if teetotal principles prevail, and suggest possible remedies; such as the "Universal Medicine," where a temperance lecturer is himself imbibing on the sly, and John Bull recovering from his watery humours and going in once more for strong beverages.

The year 1847 found "Phiz" in full working power, with commissions in plenty. In that year he produced some of his best work; "Dombey" and the "Knight of Gwynne" were both illustrated, and four other books published at the same time deserve special mention.

"Valentine McClutchy," by W. Carleton, was issued from Dublin in 1847, and it may be considered one of the books which were successful mainly because they were illustrated by "Phiz." Of the twenty there is scarcely one that is not thoughtfully designed and carefully etched. The Irish characters are depicted with certainty and knowledge, while the artistic qualities of the plates are beyond question. As in many other cases the later etchings are better than the first, for Browne seems to have taken some time to get thoroughly into accord with the letterpress. "The Widow and her dying Child" is an exquisite composition, while "The Madman expounding the Bible," "The Rent-day," "The Vulture vanquished," and "Phil hugged in a tight embrace," are all spirited and admirable work. "Solomon discourseth" and the "Rival Parsons," are examples of humour, in which "Phiz" excelled at the time.

From his earliest years of designing, "Phiz" exhibited an aptitude for illustrating hunting scenes, and achieved a fame which clung to him through life. Possessing a personal knowledge of the field, he was enabled to make illustrations of scenes he had often witnessed, and thus the eight etchings of hunting incidents in "Hawbuck Grange" (1847) are the great attraction of the volume. A novel called "The Long-lost Found" began to appear in serial form the same year. The advertisement stated that the work would probably astonish the nineteenth century, and as an almost necessary fate it never went farther than three parts. Each of these parts contained two plates by "Phiz," but their colour was poor though the drawing was fair. The last book to be mentioned as belonging to 1847 is Le Fanu's "Torlogh O'Brien," with twenty-two plates by "Phiz," most of them repulsive from their disagreeable and shocking subjects. "Garney's death by the Strappado," and the "Carousal in Con Donovan's Chamber," are both scenes far too horrid for illustration, and they are the more painful because the artist seemed to have gloried in his labour on them. "The Parting between Neville and Phene," where the gentleman woos, wins, and afterwards weds the fair Irish girl, is the most pleasing in the series.

The plates in Mayhew's "Image of his Father" (1848) are all good, and the book is an interesting specimen of "Phiz's" smaller works. "Impey amusing Hugh," "Please, ma'am, can you tell me?" "Dando devotes himself to Greece," "A Concert," and "De Vyse repenteth," are all well drawn, composed with accuracy as illustrating the text, and they are generally very well printed. The twelve etchings to Blanchard Jerrold's "Disgrace to the Family" (1848), are fairly representative of the style of "Phiz" at the time.

Mr. Ned Pepper and Mr. Augustus Tomlinson parading the Ball-room.
From "Paul Clifford."

In 1849 the "Fight of the Fiddlers," by G. P. R. James, was illustrated with twenty-one wood engravings, some of them quite small; the figure of Marian on page twenty-two is decidedly pretty. The series of Lytton Bulwer's novels, published in octavo from 1849 to 1854, embraced eight frontispieces by "Phiz." These were for "Eugene Aram," "Godolphin," "Last of the Barons," "Last Days of Pompeii," "Night and Morning," "Rienzi," "Pelham," and "Paul Clifford." They are fairly good engravings, the best being that here introduced, "Mr. Ned Pepper and Mr. Augustus Tomlinson parading the Ball-room," from "Paul Clifford."

In 1852 "The Five Senses," a set of five large prints, were published in oblong folio, 3s. 6d. plain, and 5s. 6d. coloured. The best is "Seeing," which illustrates a showman, who shouts, "Now then, gents, open your eyes, blow your precious noses, and don't breathe upon the glasses." The little "Peep at the Pixies," by Mrs. Bray (1854), contains six very nice little cuts, "The Pixies' Bath" being the best.

In 1854 Albert Smith's "Pottleton Legacy," with twenty plates by "Phiz," appeared, all being excellent. "Miss Martha Twinch's Adventure in the Wild-beast Show," "Mrs. Wracketts receives her Friends," "Tip's degradation," "The Boarding House," and "The Return from the Races," are all plates with full subjects, having many excellent figures; "Mr. Spooner meets his father," where the young spendthrift is caught in

Pallet floors a host.   From Smollett's "Peregrine Pickle."

very gay company by his father, and "The Lawyer's fate," as he tries to escape from the strong-room, are also good.

In 1857 Messrs. Routledge published a series of the older English novels, each with eight wood engravings after "Phiz," "Joseph Andrews," "Amelia," "Tom Jones," "Roderick Random," and "Peregrine Pickle" being the chief. These illustrations, though not very well engraved, are fairly representative of Browne's style in woodcuts at that period, and two of them are here introduced. "Booth in the hamper" is from Fielding's "Amelia," and "Pallet floors a host" from Smollett's "Peregrine Pickle."

"Nuts and Nutcrackers" (1857), contains a large number of etchings and small woodcuts. The latter are humorous and clever; the best being "A Nut for Domestic Happiness," and "A Nut for St. Patrick's Night," in the cuts, and "Gentlemen Jocks and Honourable Members," in the plates. In 1858 Mrs. Gatty's "Legendary Tales" was published, with four good wood engravings; but Thornbury's "Buc-

Booth in the hamper. From Fielding's "Amelia."

caneers" of the same date has six lithographic illustrations of a very ordinary kind.

Mrs. Beecher Stowe's New England tale of "The Minister's Wooing" is illustrated with thirteen etchings by "Phiz," none of them so good as his work frequently was. They show how utterly Browne failed to grasp the characteristics of the negro race, for they are here uncertain and weak, with little talent displayed in their execution. The last book to be mentioned is Ware's "Fortunes of the House of Pennyl," with six double-page cuts of a decidedly inferior quality.

"Never mind, ma'am," said the ruffian on the box, "there's a heavy goods waggon a-coming on behind." From *Judy.*

CHAPTER XI.

MISCELLANEOUS BOOKS ILLUSTRATED SINCE 1860, AND ODDS AND ENDS.

THE year 1860 has been chosen for the division of the miscellaneous books illustrated by "Phiz" chiefly because up to that time he had produced work which in the vast majority of cases was worthy of admiration; but after 1860 his illustrations become more mannered in style and execution. They gradually declined in merit until 1867, when the severe illness frequently mentioned overtook him, and from that time nothing absolutely original came from his pencil.

The prime of the artist was between the years 1840 and 1860, and from 1860 to 1880 was, broadly speaking, the period of his decline. This does not mean that everything Hablôt Browne did before 1860 was excellent nor everything since that time was bad. We have several times seen comparative failure in his earlier works as in his later there are some that will be found of very high merit.

The largest series of illustrations "Phiz" produced in the time under consideration was for the work ultimately published under the title of " Sir Guy de Guy, a stirring Romaunt," in 1864. These consisted of between fifty and sixty quarto drawings, and the artist's original idea was to publish the series by lithography as " The Adventures of Pott," with a rhyming commentary by himself. The artist carried the sketches to Mr. George Halse, and asked his advice in the matter. Mr. Halse having some experience in literary undertakings, saw at once the merits of the designs and the poverty of the accompanying verses. He suggested an alteration in the projected work, made a selection of forty from the series and, at the artist's request, wrote poetical letterpress to go with the work.* " Sir Guy de Guy " was the result, and Mr. Halse took the *nom de plume* of " Rattlebrain " for the occasion. This book was illustrated with woodcuts, which were chiefly bits from the forty selected sketches, but two or three new designs were added. The title and the scheme of the book as published were entirely Mr. Halse's, who utilised the drawings so far as possible, and when they were unsuitable the designs were altered to suit the text. The *Athenæum* at the time called the book " a remarkably brilliant example of its kind." Besides the forty cartoons, there are twenty tentative sketches for the work in Mr. Halse's possession, and several of the small designs used in this volume as initials were first drawn for " Sir Guy de Guy."

In 1862 Phiz was busy with the new graphotype process of reproducing

* Three sets of photographs of these forty sketches were printed at the time, and now belong respectively to Dr. Browne, Mr. Halse, and Messrs. Routledge.

drawings, and he published a broadside of "*The Times,* such as they are, 1862," the same size as the journal of which every Englishman is supposed to be so proud. This was profusely illustrated with humorous sketches, nearly one hundred and fifty in number—several being reproduced in this book, the tailpiece to the Preface, and the headpieces to Chapter V. and this chapter, as well as several of the smaller designs, being amongst them. In the same year "Snowflakes," by Miss M. B. Edwards, was published. It has twelve illustrations by Browne, reproduced in colour by Mr. Ed. Evans. They are of the "pretty book" order, and have little artistic merit, the colouring spoiling any charm they might otherwise have possessed.

In January, 1864, "Can you forgive her," by Anthony Trollope, was begun in monthly shilling parts, and the first volume was completed in October of the same year. Each of these parts had two etchings by Browne, but none of them were very successful. The last one, " Dear Greenhow," is quite a failure, as it does not agree with the text. In the novel Captain Bellfield and Mrs. Greenhow are described as "looking at a book of photographs which both of them were handling together," but in the plate the object they touch is a portrait in a small case. This misconception of idea irritated the author, and the second volume was given to other artists to illustrate, and instead of etchings wood engravings were given. " Tom Moody's Tales," edited by Mark Lemon, contains a frontispiece steel plate and twelve full-page woodcut illustrations, which, however, are rather poor, with the exception of the admirable trotting horse in " What Firkin picked up on the road." Another 1864 publication, the " Strange Adventures of a Gentleman," bears on the title, " With illustrations by H. K. Browne and others," but only one is signed " Phiz," and that is not very good.

About this time Browne prepared several series of hunting sketches which met with a favourable reception, and are in some cases still in the market as saleable first-hand books. The twelve lithographs of " Hunting Bits," 1862, are fair reproductions of the original drawings, though perhaps the red and green of the coats of the hunters are too brilliant, and it is noticeable that never once in the series is the object of the chase itself to be seen, though again and again it seems just outside the edge of the picture. "Dame Perkins and her Grey Mare," of the same character, referred to in Chapter VIII., was published as a coloured series in 1866, and two years later "Racing and Chasing" appeared. These fifty sketches were "engraved" by the graphotyping process, a decidedly unsatisfactory method of reproduction. "Sketches of the Seaside and the Country" are of a similar character, but less clever in conception. "London's Great Outing," 1868, and the "Derby Carnival, 1869," are sixpenny graphotype productions of scenes on the road to the Derby, embracing the same illustrations differently arranged.

"Cassell's Penny Readings" (1866) contains several careful woodcuts by "Phiz;" the best being "Mrs. Gamp's apartment," "Darby Doyle," and "Shall we make a man of him?" besides many other illustrations which make it a volume well worth possessing.

On July 14th, 1869, Browne first made his appearance in *Judy* with the cut of "A Frightful Shame." On the 21st another by him appeared, and regularly up to the time of his death he contributed to the magazine. Sometimes Browne supplied his own subject, giving the letterpress of the scene as well as the pictorial representation of it; but more often he made the drawing only, to suit the dialogue supplied by others.

Mr. Edward Dalziel, the chief proprietor of *Judy*, to whose courtesy I am indebted for the cut at the end of the preceding chapter, tells me he saw very little of Browne. Mr. Chapman introduced Mr. Dalziel to the artist and sometimes they met afterwards, but this was very seldom; for, like everyone else, Mr. Dalziel found Browne very shy and not at all communicative either personally or by letter. Mr. Dalziel, however, relates how very obliging he found Browne in their transactions, and how readily the artist would exert himself to be of service to the comic magazine when he could. Some contributions of Browne to *Judy* have been brought together in one volume,

"A Shillingsworth of Phiz;" and "Yoicks," *Judy's* sporting book, also contains a number. Both of these are popular books which still command a ready sale.

In 1871 "Agatha," by Mr. G. Halse, appeared with some etched illustrations having clear, well-engraved outlines. Its four plates are all ruled with a machine; the early impressions are good, and the wood engraved tail-pieces and initials are beautiful works of art.

"All about Kisses" (1876), with a hundred illustrations by "Phiz," ought to have been a popular book. It was compiled by Browne, and consists of a selection of quotations on the art of kissing, and whom, when, and where to salute. The cuts, though possessing a certain humour, are too roughly engraved to be admirable. In 1878 Browne made thirty-six wood engravings for "Aunt Effie's Nursery Rhymes," which, like those in the last-named book, are fairly well designed but very badly engraved.

One of the last books published with "Phiz's" illustrations is Phelps's edition of Shakespeare (1883). This is embellished with a number of full-page wood engravings after Browne's designs now in the collection of the Duchess of St. Albans. There are also many books being republished in second or later editions which contain illustrations by "Phiz," and these are likely to continue to be published for a long time to come. Messrs. Routledge, Messrs. Ward & Lock, Messrs. Chapman & Hall, and others, with all the plates in stock are frequently reprinting and issuing new editions of the popular works under their control.

Of the "Odds and Ends" produced by Browne it is quite impossible to give any detailed account. Mention has casually been made of the large numbers of sketches he prepared, and thus some idea of the overflowing nature of the artist's genius has been given. Besides these, however, there are a few which do not fall into any category, except the second title to this chapter, and yet they are too important to be passed over altogether.

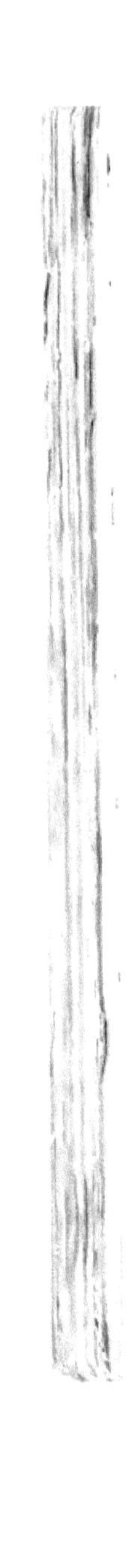

For Dr. Westall, his medical adviser, Browne several times made sketches, and presented them as much in acknowledgment of the Doctor's long attendance as in compliment to him as a friend. The plate here introduced is a fac-simile of two drawings executed to submit to the Croydon Board of Health in competition for the designs for a seal. "Hygeia," the uppermost design, is a separate drawing from the others, and is the one accepted for the seal, since prepared and still in use. "Purity," below, is a sketch for the seal first sent on approval, and those surrounding it were suggestions of a humorous character introduced as likely to amuse the committee of selection. Their bearing on the subject of the preservation of health is decidedly entertaining. "A Radish," the tailpiece to Chapter V., and "A Turnip," used in a similar way in this chapter, were both drawn about the same time as the seal, and were pictorial comments on the benefits likely to arise from the extensive system of drainage then being commenced by the Croydon Board of Health. These drawings, with several other interesting works, are now the property of Dr. Westall's widow, who has kindly placed them at my disposal for use here.

At the time of the introduction of the penny post both "Phiz" and Leech caricatured Mulready's design for a postage envelope: the two caricatures were remarkably clever and humorous, and each had points of excellence which rendered it noteworthy. They were shown in the London exhibition of the works of "Phiz."

Shortly after the appearance of "Uncle Tom's Cabin," Browne painted "Eva and Topsy" in oil colours. The subject was prettily treated though not very carefully drawn, but being likely to become popular, the picture was excellently engraved by Mr. Robert Young on a plate about 16 by 12 inches. The publication, however, was attended with "Phiz's" usual ill success when he tried independent publishing, and very few copies were sold.

Browne projected many things that came to nothing. Till he removed to Banstead he was always too busy with commissions to think out a project, and

could not spare time to bring any to completion.   It was after he was at
Banstead he published the hunting subjects, and finding they met with a
ready sale he continued their production.   "The Rivals," published as a
child's book, was also the type of a good many of his projects.   It was a
lengthy poem of a semi-burlesque nature, interspersed with songs, and
numbers of initial letters of a similar character to those used in this volume.
Although Browne had a large experience of book-illustration, he was not
practical, and the works projected as original publications were arranged
with such a supply of illustrations and on such curious proportions that they
never could have paid.   As to remodelling a book, that never occurred to him.
If it did not please the first publisher who saw it, it was most likely con-
signed to the waste-basket.   Much, therefore, has been lost of the artist's
minor work, which, though it never reached the stage of publication, need
not necessarily have been finally rejected and destroyed.

A Croydon Turnip.   From a Drawing lent by Mrs. Westall.

CHAPTER XII.

BESIDES the contributions to various academies and institutions already mentioned, there have been held two prominent exhibitions of the "Works of 'Phiz.'" The first took place in the earliest months of 1883 in the Art Club at Liverpool, and the other in The Fine Art Society's rooms in London, during the last three months of the same year.

In October, 1882, about three months after the death of the artist, the committee of the Liverpool Art Club issued a notice that they proposed to hold in the beginning of 1883 a memorial exhibition of the "Works of 'Phiz,'" under the control of a sub-committee consisting of Dr. Edgar Browne, the artist's eldest son, Mr. Philip M. Rathbone, and Mr. R. D. Radcliffe. It was asked that the exhibition should be as complete as possible, and represent satisfactorily any branch of Art in which the artist worked. It was further said, "In order to make it so, the co-operation not only of those possessing his works, but of all who have any knowledge of their whereabouts is necessary, and the committee hope the recipient of the circular will assist them in carrying out this object. Information is desired as to paintings in oil or water-colour, chalk drawings (especially a series of Irish sketches made about 1850), original drawings for book illustrations, and proofs of etchings or woodcuts."

This announcement took many people by surprise. "Phiz" was well known as a prolific illustrator, but except to his personal friends it seems to have dropped out of memory that he did anything else. Some curiosity was evinced to see the artistic other side of the inventor of Sam Weller and the immortaliser of Pickwick, and the exhibition was specially interesting from its unfolding the versatility of the artist. Even Hablôt Browne's intimate friends were agreeably surprised by the extent to which the collection swelled, and the public responding freely by attending in considerable numbers, the undertaking was a decided success.

The Liverpool exhibition contained four hundred and nine works, and was fully representative of the artist's life and labours. The principal pictures, sketches, and designs there shown are elsewhere fully described in this book. The contributors numbered fifty, the majority of whom resided in or about London.

Having been impressed with the importance of the Liverpool collection, I proposed to the directors of The Fine Art Society that a similar exhibition should be made in their galleries, and in due time the collection was opened to the London public. The rooms being smaller than those of the Liverpool Art Club, only two hundred works were displayed, but other uncatalogued pictures afterwards sent in made the collection nearly as large as that at Liverpool, and much finer in quality, as the weaker examples in water-colours were omitted. In both the London and the Liverpool collections the chief attractions, such as the Duchess of St. Albans' drawings and the oil paintings, were the same.

The freshened interest taken in the works of " Phiz," and the resuscitation of his fame, have been greatly due to these exhibitions and to the artist's sons, who worked so assiduously to get together thoroughly representative collections of their father's artistic labours.

Kit Nubbles searched for the five-pound note.   Unused block for "Master Humphrey's Clock."

CHAPTER XIII.

HINTS TO COLLECTORS OF THE WORKS OF "PHIZ."

The Collector.

IF the reader of this book has been interested in the subject with which it deals, he cannot fail to be or to become an admirer of the works of "Phiz," and therefore a collector of them so far as time and opportunity will allow.

The books that such an one will first naturally seek after are the original editions of Charles Dickens's novels, none of which fortunately are rare or beyond the reach of the majority. The volume most likely to run a high price is the "Pickwick," a fine copy of which, with the Seymour, Buss, and

x

first " Phiz " plates sometimes reaches five guineas, though, as a rule, fair copies may be obtained for half that sum; while copies with the two etchings by " Phiz " substituted for the Buss plates are always less. In the original condition with stitched covers (see p. 82), and with all the original advertisements and other dealer's extrinsic signs for enhancing values, this publication may be priced double the sum first named; but the ordinary mortal, who does not see how an advertising announcement alters the intrinsic value of a book, will be well content to obtain good impressions in a volume ready bound, even though it has not " the original monthly-part green cover."

The other Dickens volumes, " Nicholas Nickleby," " Humphrey's Clock," " Martin Chuzzlewit," " Dombey," " David Copperfield," " Bleak House," "Little Dorrit," and the "Tale of Two Cities," are equally worthy of honoured places in any library, whether specially devoted to " Phiz " or not. The " David Copperfield " and the " Bleak House " plates being the most artistically valuable, are likely in the future to be worth more in money than the others. Half the sum first quoted for " Pickwick " is a fair price to pay for any of the other novels, while occasionally a sovereign will in an auction-room command any one of these, where the etchings are only ordinary impressions. A " Dombey " with a fine copy of the " Dark Road " is fortunately not difficult to find, and when it is good all the other plates are likely to be fine also. " Sunday under Three Heads," (see p. 109) in the original edition is valuable and now difficult to find; the two reprints of it are poor, so that it is possible Messrs. Chapman and Hall may make a new edition with the original blocks, one of which is printed here at page 109. " Sketches of Young Gentlemen" and " Young Couples," (see p. 117) are also rare and well worth looking after.

" Mervyn Clitheroe," by Ainsworth (see p. 173), is a volume which contains some of the most characteristic of the work of " Phiz," but it varies greatly in the printing, and a collector should examine any offered volumes carefully before concluding a purchase. It is impossible to name any price for this book, but it is not very expensive at present, whatever it may be in the future. Ainsworth's other novels (see Chapter VI.), are not nearly so much worth possessing.

Charles Lever's stories form another series of books where "Phiz" is triumphant, and every volume is, as indicated in Chapter V., worthy of a place in any library, and of an honoured position amongst the works of Hablôt Browne. "Harry Lorrequer," "Charles O'Malley," "Con Cregan," "St. Patrick's Eve," "The Knight of Gwynne," "The Dodd Family," and "The O'Donoghue" are the best, and quite enough to make a representative selection; the last because of the amusing mistake in the title of the last plate in the earliest issue (see p. 158). Smedley's "Lewis Arundel" and "Harry Coverdale" are excellent books (see p. 180), and also were illustrated by "Phiz" with marked success. Broadly speaking, the Phiz illustrations to Lever's, Ainsworth's, and Smedley's works are as good as those in Dickens, and much cheaper in present price. Winkles' "Cathedrals" (see p. 203) is desirable as containing some of the earliest "Phiz" work; and the plate of John Gilpin, which won the Society of Arts' medal, is worthy of a frame if a well-preserved copy can be found, but that is not easily done. "Paul Periwinkle" (see p. 207), "Godfrey Malvern," by T. Miller (see p. 208), "Valentine McClutchy," by Carleton (see p. 210), "Hawbuck Grange" (see p. 211), Mayhew's "Image of his Father" (see p. 211), are all illustrated in a masterly way, and may be had for a moderate price. "Samuel Sowerby" (see p. 209) and "The Commissioner" (see p. 209) are also distinguished as containing the same plates differently titled and applied to different stories. "The Dissection of Teetotalism" (see p. 210), contains five plates of the best character, and the large oblong folio publication of "The Five Senses" (see p. 212), is a favourable specimen of "Phiz's" unaided and unguided work. "The Pottleton Legacy" by Albert Smith (p. 213), and "Joseph Fume's Paper on Tobacco" (p. 204), are also volumes with fine plates by "Phiz."

The Hunting Sketches are so characteristic of "Phiz" that no collection

can be even fairly representative without them.   "Racing and Chasing,"
"Hunting Bits," "Dame Perkins's Ride to Market," are the best, and are still
readily obtainable.   The broadsides illustrated by "Phiz" have also some of
his cleverest work, such as "*The Times*, such as they are, for 1862," with
scores of designs, and "London's Great Outing," published like a newspaper
about the same time.

Of later books Mr. Halse's "Sir Guy de Guy" and "Salad of Stray
Leaves," and *Judy's* "Shillingsworth of Phiz," are amongst the most
characteristic of the period.

All admirers of the artist will desire to obtain a specimen of his personal
work, such as a sketch in water-colour, or a chalk drawing.   His family still
possess a large number of sketches and drawings open for sale, and they are
neither difficult nor expensive to obtain through the usual dealers.   These
vary from initial letters and first ideas to large sketches and finished designs.
Drawings by "Phiz" occasionally come into the market at auctions, and,
as quoted at p. 72, they sometimes reach good prices.

A "grave hint" as a word of caution to the collector may be added.   Be
chary in believing that your own collection is the finest ever brought together.
A pretentious American collector has amused such of the London public as
have seen his publication by declaring in print that he possesses a "Phiz"
book which contains "all the sketches, several hundreds, that can be obtained,

if not all that Mr. Browne ever made," and this in the face of the well-known series of drawings and sketches in the possession of the Duchess of St. Albans and other contributors to the recent "Phiz" Exhibition.   Probably the good-natured American is only repeating what his dealer told him ; but collectors on this side of the Atlantic know full well that the statements of less responsible dealers are to be received with caution, and are never to be repeated unless the facts have been carefully inquired into and found correct.

An unpublished block prepared for "Master Humphrey's Clock."

CHAPTER XIV

METHOD OF WORK AND POSITION AS AN ARTIST.

THE methods pursued by "Phiz" in the preparation of his artistic labours are frequently, as occasion offers, commented on in previous parts of this book. On his style and manner of painting in oils and water-colours there is no necessity to say anything further; but in order to understand his procedure when engaged on his chief illustrations for books, some additional account will not be out of place.

It is not a common practice nowadays to etch either an illustration or any other subject on a polished plate of steel. Etchings in some cases, especially when required for large numbers, such as for the books "Phiz" illustrated, have been in former days worked on steel, but copper plates are now almost exclusively employed for this branch of the art of engraving. To etch on steel requires more labour and is generally more difficult than etching on copper. Copper being softer, the burin or needle more easily enters it than steel; an effect is therefore more quickly obtained on it, and the result is freer and more artistic, because more rapidly produced, and also because the printer can secure from the sympathetic copper a ground or tint that the steel will not yield. At the same time etched work on copper sooner deteriorates in the process of printing, so that before electrotyping and "steel" surfacing of copperplate was known, it was almost a necessity to etch on steel. Electrotyping by a process perfected since "Phiz" began illustrating, is employed for the multiplication of copperplate etchings, as it had been for years previously for steelplate engravings. It produces a plate, by an interesting electric process, consisting of a layer of copper deposited on the matrix, which is little inferior to the original work. Over this plate a thin coating of iron, called steel-surfacing, is thrown by another process, and this protects the soft electro copper, allowing many impressions to be taken without deterioration of the plate. But this method of duplication was never employed for the "Phiz" etchings, and when the demand exceeded the supply that could be obtained from the plates, the subjects were transferred to stone and were printed by lithography.*

When "Phiz" was engaged with the Dickens illustrations, he usually sent the sketch to the author the day following that on which he received the "copy" with the subject suggested for representation.† As there were usually two etchings in hand at one time (because two etchings appeared in each monthly part, and also because it was found commercially economical to have a plate large enough to hold two subjects, which could be printed at little more expense than one), the second sketch was sent immediately afterwards. The following table prepared by Browne himself shows exactly how much time was occupied by the etcher when in ordinary work without extreme pressure, and when etchings for other publications were also in hand. The table was prepared for the publisher's guidance as to how long the month's two etchings should take to prepare.

* The first "Phiz" plate printed in this manner was one of the "Dombey" illustrations.
† See also pages 60 to 65.

A DIARY.

Friday evening, 11th Jan. .	Received portion of copy containing Subject No. 1.
Sunday	Posted sketch to Dickens.
Monday evening, 14th Jan. .	Received back sketch of Subject No. 1 from Dickens, enclosing a subject for No. 2.
Tuesday, 15th Jan. . . .	Forwarded sketch of Subject 2 to Dickens.
Wednesday, 16th Jan. . .	Received back ditto.
Sunday	
Tuesday, 22nd Jan. . .	First plate finished.
Saturday, 26th Jan. . . .	Second ditto finished.—Supposing that I had nothing else to do, you may see by the foregoing that I could not well commence etching operations until Wednesday, the 16th.

	Tuesday	15	
		16	
		17	
		18	
		19	
	Sunday	20	
You may date from the receipt of the first sketch back from Dickens.		21	
		22	Plate No. 1 finished.
		23	
		24	
		25	
	Saturday	26	Plate No. 2 finished.
		10 days.	

I make ten days to etch and finish four etchings.   What do you make of it?

After the etching of the subject on the plate, Browne frequently sent to the assistant, who by the manipulation of acid produced the colour of the scene, a rough indication for his guidance.   This assistant also "bit-in" with acid to the requisite depth for printing the lines etched by the artist; and he had further to go over the plate afterwards with a graver and join any lines which in the etching had become broken or rotten.   Sometimes also "machine" work was employed to produce a tint of equal colour all over the plate, this being done with a special machine* which mechanically etched lines, and only required the supervision of a boy.

Machine work was employed mostly when cheap and quick plates were required, but sometimes the machine lines were manipulated with the acid so as to produce much of the effect of a mezzotint. " The Dark Road " in " Dombey " (see page 124), was the first plate that " Phiz " executed in this manner, and the beautiful result is a proof of the ease with which practised hands could master its technical difficulties. " The River " of " David Copperfield " and nine plates in " Bleak House," as well as many later subjects, were all successfully treated in the same way, and an examination of them will show the faint machined lines all over the plate. Mr. Young was Browne's assistant, or "co-partner" for the greater part of the years of " Phiz's " popularity, and the following little note, of date about 1845, is a specimen of many communications which were constantly passing between them :—

MY DEAR " CO,"—Pray help me in an emergency; put a bottle of aquafortis in your pockets, wax and all other useful adjuncts, and come to me to-morrow about one or two o'clock, and bite in an etching for me, ferociously and expeditiously. Can you? Will you?—oblige, Yours sincerely, H. K. BROWNE.

2, Stamford Villas.

Another method of work was the graphotype process, as employed for the broadside of " *The Times*, such as they are, 1862," and "London's Great Outing," and some minor designs. This was a kind of engraving or etching on zinc, which was transferred to stone and printed by lithography; but the result was unsatisfactory; and even yet, with all the improvements since added, the method, which has many names, has much to secure before attaining the perfection required for the reproduction of artistic drawings.

* Browne's machine was kept in Mr. Young's room at Furnival's Inn, and (in 1884) is still there. Browne's first idea in using the machine was probably to prevent any transference of his etchings to the lithographic stone, and for the plates in which he employed machined lines this was at first secured. Latterly, however, it has been found practicable to transfer these also to stone, and for popular editions of works containing his illustrations this transference is now frequently employed.

For Browne's publications in wood engraving he drew on the block, and in lithography he made the drawings only. From these the engravers and chromo-lithographers worked, so that there is nothing to be told specially of their method of production. This portion of our subject may therefore be concluded with the following humorous (and rhyming) letter, which has been lent for publication by Mr. F. G. Kitton, the author of a capital brochure on " Phiz " recently published.

The letter is headed with a rough pen-drawing of half a dozen hats of various kinds flying along in a high wind, with an arm and a leg appearing behind a cloud of mist, as if some one was vainly endeavouring to catch his hat. It refers to " *The Times* " broadsheet just mentioned, and inquires if each column of the paper is to be drawn separate or if one large sheet of zinc will be suitable.

              " Eureka !   *November 12, '61.*

" Hooray ! hooray ! that Mr. Jay has found my precious paper !!!! Imagine, yes imagine, pray, how I did shout and caper, and *bless* my eyes that saw it. Now, I must make haste and draw it upon zinc, and please the gods, make lots of jink. Pray will you think when Messrs. Hanhart next you see to enquire about *zincography !* if whether it were right and meet to have a plate full size of the sheet or in strips to suit each column,* to draw thereon my notions solemn ?

" Oh what a day for work, I say ! Nice rain, delicious fog !! I'm at it hard, I sweats away, I go the entire hog, and you ditto, I can tell. Good luck, and do your business well. Sell all the stock you want to sell, and trundle care off down to H—H.—Yours truly, H. K. BROWNE.

" Kind regards from me to all the family."

It is somewhat difficult to define Hablôt Browne's position as an artist in relation to his fellow labourers with pencil or needle. As the painter who began by contributing to the Westminster Hall competition and who at

---

    * The dimensions of the plates he asks about are here sketched slightly.

various times exhibited pictures at the Royal Academy, the British Institution, and other galleries, it is comparatively easy to place the modest pedestal required for him. But for the illustrator who accompanied with success the brightest novelist of the time, who never was a clog to the writer's progress and frequently a spur to his energies—the inventor of Guppy, Micawber, Sam Weller, and their associates—who interpreted Lever's, Ainsworth's, Smedley's, and a hundred others' ideas into visible form, and often rendered a book saleable which otherwise might not have found a score of subscribers, and who above all was the most artistic illustrator of his day, the position is not so readily found.

In the first place it is certain that Browne lost a great deal and was much to blame in not studying systematically from the life as well as from nature. Other artists with less than a tithe of the same artistic capacity, at first able to do common work only, have become powerful draughtsmen by careful study, and through never drawing except from the living figure. In some of these cases the charm given by genius is wanting, yet we cannot but admire their mastery over the pencil, and regret that Browne did not cultivate the same power, as he might easily have done.

It has already been mentioned that beyond the perfunctory lessons at Finden's studio, Browne received scarcely any artistic training. He went occasionally when young to classes for life study at St. Martin's Lane, but he was irregular in his attendance. A little later he belonged to the Langham Sketching Club, and he often said how much he enjoyed his evenings there. Models he very seldom employed, and twice only did he have a hired model at Furnival's Inn, and that was for an illustration to Finden's Shakespeare, with a result far from satisfactory. Finally, after 1850, it appears he never drew except from his imagination or recollection, and made no use of memoranda in the way he had sometimes done up to this time. Before 1850 he used to draw people or objects that he had seen, such as would be suitable for characters or accessories of designs, or even for backgrounds,* and through these he composed his illustrations or pictures; but after this time he trusted entirely to his inner consciousness and memory.

Browne also travelled little, so that he never understood the many great and noble works of Art that other artists have created. He did not care about seeing things in the traveller's or tourist's sense of the term; and fresh scenery had no particular attraction for him. His artistic powers therefore languished for want of proper nourishment, and though the ideas of the author he was illustrating usually supplied him with sufficient materials from which to prepare his illustration, yet his deficiency in training hampered him unnecessarily, and when his paralytic illness overtook him, his hand, which if thoroughly trained might have remained under his control, lost the greater part of its cunning.

Hablôt Browne was paradoxically both like and unlike Thomas Bewick, the father of English wood engraving. He was like him in not having been trained academically, and unlike him because he resolutely refused to study earnestly and lovingly from nature. They were like each other because both had genius for making illustrations of the highest order, combined with a humorist's love of fun whenever it could be introduced, intermingled with a strange feeling of sadness occasionally overshadowing their productions. They were unlike in so far as "Phiz" strove more to amuse than instruct, while at the same time doing both; while Bewick's desire was primarily to instruct, and his humour was only one of the means to his end.

Browne was more nearly akin in his Art to Hogarth than to any other old English painter and illustrator. He followed this master's footsteps in telling pictorial stories in chapters; and though he could not aspire to Hogarth's insight into human character, yet when the subject touched him he would

* He would, to use his own words, go "to have a look at a thing," and once when occupied with "Bleak House" he went "to have a look at" a lime-pit. He wanted to see the big crushing wheels for one of his illustrations, and this he did without leaving the rent of his trap. The result was the weird plate of "A Lonely Figure," representing Lady Dedlock in her flight.

give such suggestions of deep feeling and pathos, or jaunty humour and smiling vivacity, as revealed in him the true spirit of artistic greatness.

Grave and didactic we find "Phiz" frequently, and this phase of his genius should always be remembered; but it is as a humorist we love to recollect him—as one who carries us out of ourselves and our own circle for a time to revel with him in the rollicking fun of an Irish fair, or the comical surprises of a tyro in hunting on horseback, making us smile in spite of ourselves; and when he takes off the imbecilities of quack doctors, or the troubles of a sentimental couple, or pokes fun at a grave committee on drainage, we are charmed with the raciness, the unexpectedness, and the unfailing well of humour which bubbled up cheerfully from the beginning of his Art life to his very last drawing.

The position of "Phiz" as an illustrator is in the front rank of the workers of the middle of the nineteenth century. There are three men whose claims to the first place are yet matters of dispute. George Cruikshank and John Leech were artists of a similar character to Hablôt Browne, and both executed works which are the nearest approach to any "Phiz" designed. The latter, notwithstanding his untrained hand, was decidedly the most artistic of the three, though his modesty throughout life prevented him seeking for the recognition that was his due.

A laurel of equal merit is the most satisfactory crown for the trio, as they deserve equivalent admiration. In some respects Cruikshank surpasses both Leech and "Phiz," and in the same way Leech is occasionally ahead of "Phiz" and Cruikshank; while for readiness of pencil and power of embodying an author's ideas into pictorial representation, neither Leech nor Cruikshank, nor indeed any other illustrator of former or present days, surpasses Hablôt Knight Browne.

Letter from Charles Dickens to Hablôt Knight Browne, to which " Phiz " has added a few words and a sketch showing his joy at the termination of the work.

GENERAL INDEX.

INDEX TO WORKS

ILLUSTRATED BY "PHIZ"

DESCRIBED OR ALLUDED TO IN THE VOLUME, BEING A LIST OF BOOKS CONTAINING
IMPORTANT ENGRAVINGS BY HABLÔT KNIGHT BROWNE.

*** In this Index-Catalogue, the books marked with an asterisk (*) are volumes containing works by "Phiz" which have not been considered of sufficient importance to be described in the letterpress.

The figures placed after names or books refer to the pages in this work where they are mentioned or described.